THE SENSE OF WONDER

Also by Matthew Salesses

Craft in the Real World

Disappear Doppelgänger Disappear

The Hundred-Year Flood

I'm Not Saying, I'm Just Saying

Different Racisms: On Stereotypes, the Individual, and Asian American Masculinity

The Last Repatriate

THE SENSE OF WONDER

A Novel

MATTHEW SALESSES

Little, Brown and Company
New York Boston London

The events and characters in this book are fictitious. Certain real locations and public figures are mentioned, but all other characters and events described in the book are totally imaginary.

Little, Brown and Company
Hachette Book Group
1290 Avenue of the Americas, New York, NY 10104
littlebrown.com

First Edition: January 2023

ISBN 9780316425711
LCCN 2022934097

Printing 1, 2022

LSC-C

Printed in the United States of America

For my kids

Coaches have said recruiters, in the age of who-does-he-remind-you-of evaluations, simply lacked a frame of reference for such an Asian-American talent.

—Mark Viera, *New York Times*

PART ONE
WON

I. A JOKE ABOUT WONDER

Let me tell you a basketball joke. It's the dirtiest joke I know, because it's the truest. I heard it from Robert Sung, but since he was covering the team then, what I said was, "Your mic on?" And he said, "Off the record, just between us two gooks."

The joke goes like this: An Asian American basketball star walks into a gym. No one recognizes him, but everyone stares anyway. They've never seen an Asian so big before. They just have to know the size of his dick.

2. HIGH SCHOOL ROMANCE

I got to know Robert Sung pretty well in the end, and the key to him was what he was like in high school. In high school, he was the second-best baller on a team that won three straight New York State championships—and he got none of the credit. That lack of credit became the defining story of his life. In other words, in the story of his life, he was a subplot.

When we met, Sung was ESPN's beat writer for the New York Knicks. I had just signed with the Knicks after two years on the Clippers bench, after two years All-Ivy in college and one year as conference MVP. Sung had grown up wanting to be the first Asian American basketball star; I was the only Asian American in the NBA. In other words, people often compared us. We were the same height (six two), both point guards, and—most importantly to this story—had both played with the same superstar, Powerball! (né Paul Burton), captain of the Knicks and perennial favorite for MVP, though he never won.

I had grown up watching Powerball!, copying his moves; Sung had grown up playing in PB's shadow. I was five years younger, but since Powerball! had gone pro after one year of college, he was in his eleventh year in the league and I was in my third. Sung had been covering the Knicks for four years.

They had a strange relationship: Powerball! had everything Sung ever wanted in life, both professionally and personally—even the woman Sung loved, Brit Young, who had been with Powerball! since high school. Despite that rivalry, Sung was Powerball!'s biggest advocate, his press cheerleader. He argued endlessly that Powerball!'s reputation (as a great individual player who could never lead his team to a championship) was unfair. Powerball! had won championships in high school and college—Sung blamed the Knicks' playoff woes on the owner's bad decisions. To me, Sung's obsession seemed unhealthy—on the other hand, obsession paid his bills. (Journalists are truly terrifying people.) He wrote about Powerball! because he got money to write about Powerball!

But also, if you envy someone, it's only natural to want everyone to think they are the best. How embarrassing to envy someone just okay.

Sung knew Powerball!'s winning instinct firsthand. On their shared high school team, Sung had done the dirty work. He had taken what the offense had given him and still had managed eighteen and five. He had what TV announcers call "hustle," which is what they say when a player does more on the court than in their limited imaginations. In high school, Sung seemed destined for a Division I scholarship, four years of points and girls and being the hottest Asian on campus, if not a shot at the league. Then halfway through his senior season, he blew out his knee. He kept the ball on a crucial play and came down from the winning layup on someone's foot—Powerball!'s. The knee required surgery, and Sung missed the rest of the season. Yet that didn't stop the team from winning a third straight state championship. Scouts rated Powerball! the top high school player in the nation. Sung's scholarship prospects dried up. He landed in Division II, where he was overplayed and reinjured his leg, ending his career.

I met Sung before my season in New York even started. The Knicks had invited me to play on their summer league team as a kind of try-out, and afterward, they signed me to a one-year nonguaranteed contract. I crashed with a teammate while I looked for an apartment, but I wasn't sure I would last in New York. The only articles about the signing implied that my role on the team was to sell jerseys to New York Asians. I represented a new market. All I could do for myself was focus on the one thing I controlled: training.

When Sung called me, I was at the practice facility with one of the team's shot coaches. I didn't know how Sung got my number, unless he had access to the team contact list, but I said I would text when I was done. After my shower, I texted him that I could meet wherever he wanted. Immediately someone knocked at the door.

I jumped. I mean—it was weird timing, I didn't actually think it was him. The practice facility was an hour from Manhattan.

I pulled on my sweats and opened the door. A tall Asian guy tried to peek past me.

"Can I help you?" I asked.

"It's me."

I had never seen him before.

"Robert Sung." He reached out his hand. "I just texted you."

My spine fucking tingled.

When I recovered, I had a good look at him. He was still in basketball shape, as tall as me but stockier, maybe 220, freakishly broad-shouldered. He was good-looking—they sometimes put him on TV—with these tender, droopy eyes, single-lidded; a high nose bridge; and dense hair cut above his eyebrows. It was a real puppy-dog look, but it worked for him. He bounced on his toes, hyped, eager. Despite my wariness, this moved me. No reporter had been so excited to see me since college, maybe not even then.

He craned his neck and peered into the locker room—that was when he confided in me his dream to be the first Asian American basketball star, when he saw we were alone. I could tell he was trying to convince me that he was on my side. I wasn't immune to the connection. It was lonely being the only Asian American in the league and hardly ever getting off the bench. Maybe for the first time, I recognized just how lonely I was, and just how much it might help to talk to someone else who understood what it was like. Sometimes you don't know how alone you are until you realize you don't have to be alone.

But the connecting part was over.

Sung peered past me again and said, "I heard Powerball! would be back today. Is he in there? I really need to see him."

I said he wasn't there, I hadn't seen him. My voice shriveled.

"We were high school teammates, you know," Sung said. "I was literally in your position. He would really want to see me, I mean, if he's in there and just pretending not to be?"

What was even creepier than a stranger driving an hour to see me? A stranger driving an hour to pretend to see me.

I should have known then that Powerball! would always be Sung's main subject, that Sung would consider anyone else the same as himself: a subplot.

3. LOVE AT FIRST SLIGHT

After that first meeting, Sung kept inviting me out. Maybe he felt bad that we had started on the wrong foot. I made up excuses not to join him, but eventually we ran into each other. An old college friend had starred in an Asian American film, and one of our mutuals had tickets to the premiere. I had already committed to going when Sung texted. For whatever reason—maybe I didn't want to share anything Asian with him—I told him I wasn't interested in a movie just because it was Korean. I wanted him to catch my drift.

The venue was an old arts center in Midtown with a theater room that could seat maybe 150 and a larger ballroom for the reception. I convinced my friend to sit in the back row. The film was a rare look at small-town Asian America, and still it managed to be clichéd. Our actor friend played a son who moves back in with his Korean mom after his white dad dies. To help overcome their grief, he convinces his mom to start a restaurant together—but lo and behold, the neighbors they have known for years want nothing to do with them now. The son has to go door to door, smiling, reminding them of old relationships. When the restaurant finally starts doing okay, a white guy in a ski mask breaks in and, in the middle of robbing the place, kills the mom.

I was disappointed, but the audience gave the film a standing ovation. We were an Asian American crowd starved for representation.

At the reception, the mutual friend and I caught up with the actor, David Yoo. As the three of us chatted about the good old days, Sung appeared.

I felt bad for lying to him, but we didn't know each other. On the other hand, once the season got underway, he would cover every Knicks game for the largest sports website in the world. I had to be smart. I pretended to be glad to see him. I said I had decided to go to the premiere after all, and I introduced him to my friends.

This was the kind of person Sung was: he asked David Yoo why the guy had chosen to do such a shitty movie.

I nearly choked on my drink.

"Excuse me?" David said. His face got red—or redder, since he had the Asian flush. "You know this fucker, Won?"

"He writes for ESPN," I said, hoping that would buy me enough time to get Sung away from him.

"You've got too much talent to waste it on that kind of movie," Sung said.

I pulled his arm.

He yanked it back, and his hand knocked into someone's drink.

A woman gave a small gasp. David swore and jumped back. His eyes flashed. I remembered why we hadn't liked him much in college. He had yelled at one of the women in our friend group over a C-plus project—despite saying nothing to the other members, all male. After that, he orbited the group awkwardly. I wondered how I could forget that, what that forgetting said about me.

A little of the woman's champagne had spilled on David's suit.

It wasn't a big deal. He just wanted someone to dump on. Sung said something to me, but I was no longer paying attention. I was holding David back. He pointed at the woman and said she better not be a reporter too, because what he was about to do to her was off the record. Before we could find out what he meant, she threw the rest of her champagne at his face.

Without thinking, I jumped in front of the drink as if to take the charge.

It turned out to be the best possible thing I could have done. With my face wet, Sung was apologetic; David Yoo shut up. The woman pulled me out of the reception and helped me dry off.

As she dabbed a napkin on my forehead, I stared at her catlike eyes, her sharp chin, the deep groove of her philtrum. The truth was she had made a strong impression on me from the start, even before her drink hit me. For one, she was tall, maybe six feet. I liked tall women. Most ballers did. Then there was the sleeveless navy jumpsuit she wore that showed off how buff her arms were. I liked strong women too. She had the presence of someone confident and she spoke in short, direct clips, not mincing words. "If you stare at me like that," she said, "I might think you're hot for me. Who are you and why did you do that?"

We introduced ourselves. Won Lee. Carrie Kang. She was a producer for some big studio looking for more Asian American talent. When I asked how she got into the business of representation, she told me a memory from an early trip to Korea, channel surfing at her halmoni's house and seeing Koreans on every station—the first time she had recognized this reality as possible. Before that trip, she had thought Korean TV was something on bootlegged DVDs and at Korean restaurants. (We all have a story like this, an origin story about the first time the world showed us our own reflection.)

"The film sucked," she said. "Still, I was going to tell that asshole he did a good job. I was going to get his number. You saved me."

She added: "Get his number for a future project, not a date."

"Not a date?" I asked.

"No."

"You're single?" I asked.

"Don't make this so awkward." She laughed deeply, like she had a lower register hidden somewhere inside her. It was that, but it was also her smile. Her eyes curved into small arches, small rainbows, and both cheeks dimpled.

I wanted to see those dimples again. And again.

Later, Sung would claim that he was the reason Carrie and I got together.

4. ORIENTAL

Before my first practice with Powerball!, Sung sent me a list of advice.

1. PB prefers the ball either at the elbow or the wing.
2. If the elbow, fade to the opposite elbow and sit for a kick-out three.
3. If the wing, set a screen, then cut to the hoop and draw your man to the weakside corner.
4. PB sits on the wings when he's tired. He's using himself to spread the D. Drive or feed the post.
5. Look to PB first. You will see the flow he sees.

In other words: *Move, bitch, get out the way.*

Powerball! was my college idol. I modeled my game after his. I wore his sneakers. He played the way I wished to play: with nearly no subterfuge, just taking it to his man again and again, both of them knowing he couldn't be stopped. He was a natural three but could play any position. He could handle like a one, catch and shoot like a two, spread the floor like a three, post up like a four, even hit the boards as a five on a small-ball team meant to run.

That first day, I was eager to prove myself to him. I wanted his respect—Powerball!'s respect would mean the team's respect, and I didn't want to spend another season on the bench. The NBA puts its faith in winning, in *ball don't lie* and *talent will show,* and I still believed then that if I gave us a better chance of winning, I would play.

Not even ten minutes passed before Powerball! compared me to Sung. I frowned, and he said he didn't mean it "Oriental-like," he meant how we approached the game. I wasn't a rookie—I knew "approached the game" was nonsense. We were shooting around, and at the O-word, my hand slipped, and someone called out "Airball," to scattered laughter. I forgot about my plan to make them like me. My hands burned. I signaled for another ball, took a few steps back behind the three-point line, and swished it, then took another few steps back and swished a longer shot. Powerball! walked up beside me and made the same shot, stepped back a few more feet, and hit that one too. You could feel the attention stop around us like traffic around a car accident. Soon it became a game of horse. Powerball! hit wild shots: standing out-of-bounds, double-clutching, and arcing the ball over the corner of the backboard. Someone fucking oohed and aahed after every shot. Somehow I kept hitting them too. We matched each other basket for basket. I got that feeling that comes sometimes, like I couldn't miss, and with each make, the team extended a little more respect toward me. Five, six shots, and they held their breath, waiting to see if I could do it again. I held my breath too.

Finally, Coach blew the whistle. A few guys groaned. I thought Coach would make us run, which was what my college coach would have done if two of us had battled like that in practice. Coach called scrimmage. He said we could settle up, see what all we could do. He had a reputation in the league as a players' coach, someone who let the players do almost whatever they wanted.

We picked sides. Powerball! knew the team well and I did not. It became obvious that the scrimmage was stacked against me. But I had just spent two years on the bench, and I had to change that in New York. Otherwise, what was the point of signing? Coach blew the whistle, and I slapped my hands on the floor. Most of the guys, even the ones on my squad, sneered like, "Man, it's the first day," but Powerball! grinned, stole the initial pass, and dunked. He talked shit.

There was only one thing to do. I went down the other end and dunked too. The same asshole oohed my basket now, probably surprised I could get up that high. I thought I saw Powerball! smile.

It was just like horse. Their side would score and ours answer. The difference was a scrimmage puts bodies on the table. I had to bang around in the paint to score, while Powerball! sailed over people. I felt whatever respect I had earned slip away. No one wanted to get beat up in practice—it was practice. Finally, Powerball! waved my defender off and guarded me himself. He played me tight. For the first time, I understood what it felt like when you could see where you wanted to go and just couldn't get there, like someone trapped behind glass in a movie. I was the hero trying to save that person and I was the person who couldn't be saved. I struggled to keep the ball from Powerball!'s reaching arms, but I didn't want to pass. I stepped hard right, and he slid in front of me. I crossed left, and he slid back. Finally, I put my head down and charged him. I couldn't get free. I lifted my arm by reflex. My elbow landed in his chest.

Coach blew the whistle. We were playing no fouls, so it surprised us. It was true I had hit Powerball! hard. Powerball! didn't seem pissed though. He said, "Coach, fucking lay off the whistle."

Coach called the end of practice.

Afterward, Coach pulled me into an empty room. I, too, wanted to talk about what had happened. He could see that I had outplayed everyone except Powerball! If he had watched the summer league, then he had seen me lead the team in scoring, assists, steals, free throws, and three-point percentage.

Coach said: "Pull that kind of stunt again and I'll cut you."

My excitement vanished.

"That shit could have ended our season before it even started," he said. "Don't you ever go after PB like that."

"I wasn't trying to hurt him." That was the truth.

"You think you proved something today?" Coach's face grew white and swollen, like he was chewing on a bunch of marshmallows and storing extras in his cheeks. "You proved you belong on the end of the bench. That's it. You proved you can't be trusted."

I had taken on one of the best players in the world and nearly equaled him. My college idol. I wanted to feel good about that, about the smile Powerball! gave me, especially after the comparison to Robert Sung.

"You're a fourth-string point guard," Coach said. "Nothing more."

I started to scoot out my chair, to hold on to that feeling before it was gone.

"Stay seated," he said.

We were both grown men. He looked at me like I had to do whatever he said to do. Did I?

I didn't think he could tell me not to stand up and walk out and save my joy. On the other hand, he held my contract in his hands, he held my money, he held my future.

I sat there.

"Fourth-string point guard," he said again.

I sat there until everyone had left the locker room.

When I got back home, I searched for footage of Sung's college games. I couldn't find any. None of the regular-season games had been televised, and his career ended before the postseason tournaments. I couldn't find his high school games either. But I knew I didn't play like him. There was no way. I knew we were not the same. He had burned out in Division II ball, and whatever else, I had made the NBA. I had made my dream come true, hadn't I?

5. DISAPPEAR DOPPELGÄNGER DISAPPEAR

Carrie and I hit it off, but we were both away a lot, so we agreed to an open relationship. It was her idea: she had been in one before. She said when we were together, we would be together, and when we were apart, we wouldn't expect each other to act like we were together. That was how she put it. After that, it seemed like a contradiction to move in with her—which I did in late October—but she had found out I was sleeping on my teammate's couch and insisted. That was how she was. Neither of us had to prove anything to the other.

As the season got going, Sung and I worked things out. After all, we saw each other almost every other day. It helped that he and his wife Ducky got along with Carrie and me as couples. We went out to eat a few times, we took a ferry ride. Yet I never got as close to Sung as I might have if we had started on better terms. There was always some tension between us. If you believed Carrie, it was because me and Sung were in a love triangle—with Powerball!—a bromance.

But that was just a joke.

Whenever I wondered what made Sung so insecure or why his values seemed so strange, I kept coming back to his adoption and the fact that he was brought up by white people. Carrie thought this was unfair. Adoption was something she knew better than I did—like Sung, her mom was adopted from Korea, though after college, her mom had moved back and relearned the language, then married a Korean man, started a family, and raised her kids in America with everything she had missed as a girl. Sung refused to ever step foot in Korea again. That was the difference between us: being Korean grounded me; it unsettled and scared him. When I was around him, race seemed even more complicated. That feeling bothered me, yet it also made me give him more chances than I would have. I felt responsible, if not for causing his pain, at least for bearing witness to it.

Over many conversations, during which Sung would let slip a detail or two at a time as if he wasn't dying to talk about it, I pieced together his origin story. This is what I know:

According to his adoptive parents, Robert Sung had been abandoned as a baby at an orphanage in Seoul, with a note stating only his birthday. When he was two years and four months old, he was adopted by a white American couple. They were looking particularly for an Asian orphan. It was a Catholic belief that heathen babies needed saving from their birth countries, and also that lighter babies were more worth saving than darker ones. Encouraged by his parents to feel always both orphan and son, young Sung became sullen and sensitive. His parents were the kind of white folks who never *show* emotion, only take it out on each other. If Sung cried, his father would give him something to cry about. His mother would watch in silence and then act as if nothing had happened. When Sung confronted her, his mother said that he was making things up, he had only received a light spanking. The disappearance of his father's violence frightened Sung the most: that his reality could so easily vanish. One night, his mother burned their family's Bibles and ran off with the money from the safe. In response, Sung's father beat him more, harder. Finally, Sung followed his mother's lead; he spent his nights in shelters, his afternoons and weekends on the courts, lost and alone. In places with few Asians, he was often told to "go back to his country," and he wondered again and again where that was. He was thirteen and his own nationality. In the end, a teacher noticed his situation and arranged for him to be sent to boarding school. His father felt it worth the money to get the boy out of his sight.

From that traumatic childhood, Sung carried two inheritances. The first was a gold-nibbed pen he always had with him. If he got nervous or if an interview went in a direction he didn't like, he would take out the pen and click it. The one time I asked about the pen directly, he said only that it had been his dad's—his teeth ground together as if to stop him from saying more. I wondered whether other players figured out what his clicking meant, whether it was useful to him without him knowing. I didn't think he himself realized what he was doing.

The other inheritance was psychological. He acted as if his life was still conditional, as if at any moment, someone might send him back to an orphanage in Korea. At least, that's how I saw it. He never stopped worrying that his reality might disappear. I knew this feeling too, because part of our reality was the same: Asian American basketball player. His worry was justified. His career had fallen apart as easily as his knee. But I still had a chance. I could still make it.

6. DEBTS

In college, Sung claimed, when his knee finally went out for good, it was a relief. He could blame the injury both for the end of his career and for Brit's decision to love someone else. He became a normal college student, learning a field of study, accumulating debt, not knowing what to do with his life. Writing saved him. He majored in journalism and became a sportswriter—in this way, he continued to be a part of the team, writing about his former teammates for the school paper. He went to parties, hooked up, fell in love. Though the white woman he ended up with was surely a stand-in for Brit. They met in a "writing group," which sounded more like group therapy, and grew close by sharing their trauma. They were the type of couple who knew each other's weaknesses better than each other's strengths. Ducky, which was her nickname—a fact that always stitched me—was a high-strung Irish Catholic who talked with her hands, always had one too many drinks, and turned sarcastic when she did. To me, she seemed cartoonish, like a Charlie Brown-type character. She was short and messy and always wore bright red glasses that matched her hair. Instead of yellow fever, Asian fetish, Ducky had the kind of whiteness that *looks past* race. In other words, she thought of anyone she loved as white—maybe that was what Sung found so attractive. The one thing that didn't fit in Ducky's cartoon was her job: she taught kindergarten and loved it. She could calm a screaming child with a wink.

It's not that I didn't like her: she was bright and energetic. I simply couldn't take her seriously. I had dated a white woman in college who turned out to be racist—she had told me she didn't see why calling my roommate a thug was a problem, since he was the one who was Black, not me—and I *still* felt ashamed that I had slept with her. It had been a lesson to me: there was no such thing as a sexual relationship without race. And Ducky was most suspect when she talked about Powerball!

She did have her reasons to dislike him though. She knew about Sung's old crush on Brit, and on top of that, she knew why Sung had started writing about Powerball! in the first place. It happened like this (or so I heard from Carrie, who heard from Ducky herself): A gossip rag reported that Powerball! was cheating on Brit with a stripper, and Brit called Sung for help. She had seen Sung's writing, plus he had the authority of someone who had known them for a long time. Sung, after some investigation, broke the news that Powerball! was being blackmailed. It was a big deal and it put Sung on ESPN's radar.

You could almost chalk up that article to Sung helping out a couple of old friends—except, after that article, he kept writing about Powerball! He never stopped.

I saw the first sign of dysfunction in Sung and Ducky's private life on the very first day of the Wonder, which was what they called it when I became a star, punning on my name. I had finally gotten off the bench and had gone off for twenty-five to lead the team to its first win in eleven games. It was the best feeling I ever had in my life. But in the postgame interview, Coach acted like he had seen my talent and given me the chance, when really he had just given up. He took credit after sitting me all season. I couldn't say a thing against him or I would look ungrateful. I heard myself say I was just as surprised as anyone and was trying to enjoy the moment. It was as if the role required those lines, as if I had been given a script and had to follow it. I hated saying it. One of the reporters asked if I had heard my nickname—he said Twitter was calling me the Wonderkid. "What do you think, Won-derkid?" he asked. "Do you like it?"

He was a short white guy who unbuttoned his sport shirt one button too far. He was obviously baiting me.

"Listen," I said.

Coach kicked me under the table. I tried to adjust my expression, if it was bad enough that Coach had noticed.

"Won-derkid," the reporter said again. "Kind of cute, isn't it?"

A few of his colleagues cringed, out of disgust or embarrassment, but didn't speak up. I bit the inside of my lower lip the way I used to do in college when fans would chant "Internment" at me.

Finally, someone asked Coach if I would start the next game, saving me. That was Robert Sung. "After a game like that, he's got to be the starter, right?"

"We'll see," Coach said.

"You're not starting him?" Sung pushed. "Can I ask why not?"

"There's a good chance, but we have to explore all our options."

"How much chance?" Sung asked. "Ninety percent?"

It surprised me that Sung would keep the pressure on. It was a challenge, that "How much chance?" My heart pounded harder than when I had stepped on court.

Coach said he would start me if nothing changed on the injury list by tomorrow.

After the game, Sung and Ducky took me out to a late dinner. I felt supported by them, like maybe we would be real friends after all. Carrie had left as soon as the game ended—she had to catch a red-eye to Korea to oversee the filming of her latest TV project. I didn't have anyone else in the city I was really close with, and the mutual friend I had gone to the film premiere with had turned out to be an asshole.

In the restaurant, we were nearly mobbed by Knicks fans. One said Twitter was going wild. People ran up and high-fived me. First my oldest sister texted, then the middle one, then the youngest. It was the start of a two-week period when almost everyone in New York—even white people—wanted me to sign their shirts or hats or take photos with them. By dessert, I felt sated, joyful, like my time had at last arrived... I was glad Sung was there to see it. It had been his dream too, even if, in the end, it hadn't happened for him.

Ducky was restless, though, pissed at him for something or, at the very least, suspicious. I hadn't paid enough attention, too drunk and happy. The waiter brought a round of shots someone sent from another table. At midnight, the place would turn into a karaoke bar. I suggested we stay and sing.

Ducky sneered and said, "Robert doesn't do karaoke."

Sung's face fell.

She said, "You want to know why?"

He stated her name, cautiously. The mood became a white fog.

I said we could do something else, go somewhere else, whatever. I didn't care about karaoke that much.

"Robert doesn't do karaoke because it's too Asian," Ducky said. "Believe that?" She laughed silently.

I didn't know what to make of this. I didn't want the night to turn back into a pumpkin. In the Cinderella story, it isn't actually Cinderella who changes; the world changes and finally recognizes her.

"Let's go to the club the team is at," I said. "I'll let you in on a little secret, get you past the doormen. One of the bartenders there is a fan of mine, has been since before I even got here. The one white girl in New York with any faith."

Ducky stood and grabbed her bag. All through dinner, she had taken digs at any woman who turned to photograph us or came up to talk. She had even said one of the prettier white women by the window had "fair-weather Asian fetish," like yellow fever for opportunistic fans. At the time, I had thought it was just a bad joke.

"I didn't mean to call you faithless, Ducky," I said, trying to appease her.

Sung said we could go to a new boba place nearby; he had heard it was open late.

"I promise the club will be more fun," I said. "No karaoke."

He coughed for about five seconds.

Whether it was the alcohol or the sudden chill, I felt woozy. Sung refused to look at me. I had the feeling that, whatever Ducky suspected, she was right about him.

In a tone clearly meant to be a warning, Ducky said, "Robert is not a club person."

An hour later, I was in bed in Carrie's condo, a two-bed in Flushing far enough into Queens to be affordable, in the heart of everything Korean and a direct subway trip to the Garden. It was too far for me, really, especially from the practice facility, but it beat crashing with teammates or renting an apartment that I would have to vacate if the Knicks decided they didn't want me anymore.

That night, that game, was the first time it felt like I might get a real contract at the end of the season. I should have still been out celebrating. Instead, I lay in my pajamas in an empty condo, as if Sung's shame was contagious. The TV played some show about

British baker folk, which I watched anthropologically, as a life I knew nothing about. My phone buzzed.

WTF bro, Sung texted. Why u have to say that about ur fan?

You ruined my big night, I texted back. I got out of bed and made myself a gin and ginger. Outside the kitchen/dining room window, the lights of Queens sparkled.

Ducky doesn't trust my yellow peril ass, Sung texted.

Neither do I.

She thinks I'm cheating on her.

So that was what it was. Are you?

Sung texted me a photo of his middle finger. Don't b pissy, he added.

I added more gin to my drink and downed it.

It's still ur big night. He sent some champagne emojis and a basketball.

I felt implicated in his love problems, though, as if I, too, was cheating, even if I was in an open relationship. I knew that other reporters, and even my teammates, who had known him longer than they had known me, automatically associated me with him. Maybe I felt like I had to protect him from what people thought about me. I had to stay in and not do anything stupid, or else he would be blamed. Or maybe it was just survivor's guilt—no different from the feeling I got around other Asian Americans who'd grown up, like him, with few Asian friends or family. Guilt that I had felt at home in the same world that hurt them, that hurt us.

7. THEY CALLED IT THE WONDER

At the beginning of the season, I was the fourth point guard off the bench. The media said the Knicks didn't even need four point guards, since everything went through Powerball! anyway. Hence the theory that I was there for jersey sales. Coach didn't like me and seemed to share this theory. It was that way through the end of December. But in January, the starting point guard reaggravated an old injury, and his backup got suspended for pot, and the third guy was a rookie who never panned out. By February, trying to do everything for the team, Powerball! threw out his back. Coach was forced to play me.

Fact was I had been a star all my life. I had overcome the same racism over and over to be one. I dominated high school ball, yet college coaches passed on me because, as one recruiter said, there wasn't a "frame of reference" for me. By then, I already had plenty of frames of reference for what he meant. My older sisters were pissed. My dad was practical. He wanted me to accept his frame of reference and become an engineer. He didn't have a frame of reference for the NBA, but he did know plenty of Korean American engineers. What a person does with his life is about what he is led to believe is possible. I took the one athletic scholarship I got, to Princeton, made All-Ivy my junior and senior years, carried my team to two conference championships and then into the NCAAs, scored thirty-five in a loss on national TV, and went undrafted. I tried out and outplayed every guard I faced in summer league, then signed with my hometown Clippers, where I sat on the bench for two seasons, making a little over five grand a game (more money than I had ever seen in my life) and growing bitterer and bitterer. After I had another dominant stint in summer league, New York signed me as a marketing strategy.

After all that, the chance I got was more like a Hail Mary. Coach claimed that he had given me an opportunity, but really, he had no other options. The team was tanking. With Powerball! hurt, fans abandoned ship. The owner said he would change coaches if we didn't make the playoffs. When I got into the game, I did the same thing I had done my whole career: I played as if my life depended on each play, because it did. The team had lost all confidence, was an underdog by a dozen points at home, and I knew I had to step into the game already, as they say, on fire... and as usual, the fire I had was anger. Possession by possession, I turned that fire into a win. I scored and scored, and slowly my teammates believed in me. Because of Sung, Coach named me the starter for the next game, and I went in hyped and put up thirty-two for our second win in a row, and after that, Powerball! said Coach should just keep riding me, and Sung wrote a profile of me as the only Asian American in the league, and I scored thirty-five for a third win, and the NBA named me Eastern Conference Player of the Week, and then it was four straight wins, then five, and then, in the sixth, I got the ball with three seconds left and hit the deciding shot, and my sisters called screaming with pride, and Carrie and I had amazing sex, and the media called it the Wonder.

Everywhere I looked, reporters gathered, the team made millions from sales and endorsements, Coach came off as a genius.

After the seventh win, articles even came out that the team was better with me as its star than with Powerball!, and I smiled for the cameras and said, on the record, that I had never, ever, been overlooked.

Yet we had to lose sometime. People compared the Wonder to a fairy tale, and like a fairy tale, the trouble was the ever after. After those seven wins in a row, we had one more game before Powerball! would return. In a way, that game was the most important. An eighth straight win would mean that the team I led without Powerball! would be undefeated—forever. If we lost only *after* Powerball! came back, the Wonder would never stop. Reporters could still write their bullshit articles about how we were better without a first-ballot Hall of Famer. If we lost *before* Powerball! came back, then the next time we won, he would be the reason we won again. It was the difference between adding Powerball! to our new dynamic and adding me to the old one.

From the start, I had the rock in my hands. First I hit a jumper from the elbow. On our next possession, I found an opening and drove. Then I crossed my man over and hit a three in his face. I scored our first seven points and assisted for nine. In less than three minutes, we were up six. It looked like the streak would continue. The crowd was as loud as it ever got. The other coach called time to quiet it, and the fans cheered through the whole thirty seconds. On our bench, Powerball! pretended to bow down to me, without any trace of ill feeling. The team spent half the time-out slapping one another on the back. I felt relieved that I was still invincible. It was like seeing safe haven in front of me after a long and perilous journey.

By halftime, I had twenty-two. The court was wide open. A sort of diagram appeared in my head. Before the Wonder, I had practiced mostly with the other backups, so I had only two weeks to feel out the starters (minus Powerball!). Finally, I seemed to see us from the top down, the way the court looks when the only thing is basketball and the people we try so hard to be in life ease their demands on who we are. I would body-fake, step around a guy, and be right at the hoop; or jab-step and pull up over a too-late hand; or bounce off a screen, find daylight, and spot the open man. I hadn't ever, not even in high school, felt this clicked in, like I directed nine men, not four. Everything worked. Even Coach got into it, spinning his clipboard as I brought up the ball as if to give up drawing plays. The defense tried to adjust, but that made everyone else more open. Scoring felt like simply counting the animals as they waltzed into Noah's ark: twenty-six, twenty-eight, thirty. Maybe that was how Powerball! felt all the time.

Yet as I hit shot after shot, I got so into the flow of the offense that I forgot that the other team was scoring, too. It seemed like we were far ahead, while the scoreboard showed a close game. And then a strange thing happened: the other team seemed to have the same realization, that no matter how much I had my way, it didn't make as much difference to them as it did to me. I felt my teammates' impatience for the buzzer. I still statted with ease and got them the ball too, but it was as if we were running a race that, the farther we ran, grew shorter for our opponents...and when I looked up, I was making a shot to get *us* within two. It was crushing, the certainty that my best wasn't enough. It felt so callous and unjust. I couldn't transcend myself.

The next game, Powerball! would come back, and despite the new friendship between us, he would never put the team in my hands again.

8. CHOPPING POST, TRADING BLOCK

After the buzzer, I headed automatically toward the on-court reporter before I realized she was talking to the star of the winning team. In just seven games, I had gotten used to that mic without even knowing how much I would miss it.

Coach wanted to meet before the postgame interview. At the beginning of the Wonder, my agent had gone into contract mode, saying it was my duty to him to turn my big chance into big money, since he had taken me on without any frame of reference, and I knew what he would tell me to do if I wanted to get paid. I wanted to sneak out and go straight to eat; I craved barbecue, red meat, anything bloody—my sisters call it tiger nom-ing—but I followed Coach into an open room.

"I'm your best friend on this team," Coach said as I shut the door. It pissed me off that he wanted to meet now: not after any of the last seven wins but after our one loss. It was just like that first practice, when I put my elbow in Powerball!'s chest by accident. I wiped the sweat through my hair; I wanted Coach to smell it. "You done more than anyone ever expected. You came out of nowhere! You're a star, a media freaking phenom."

He resented me for saving his job.

"I'm just taking the open shot," I said.

"I'm designing those open shots."

I smiled and said I did not feel overlooked.

"You're going to have a lot less of those open shots now," Coach said with an emphasis on the *now.* "That won't surprise you, right? You wouldn't put a contract before the team?"

He meant that I should stop putting up the kind of numbers that would get me paid for the first time in my life.

"I want to win," I managed. "Powerball! is the star." If I didn't do what Coach wanted, he would just cut my playing time, and with no PT, I wouldn't get any numbers anyway.

He waited.

I swallowed, and my heart stuck in my throat. "I'm a team player," I said. "I'll do whatever the team needs me to do."

"I knew you would say that. Now go out and tell those vultures what you told me, and everything will be fine."

"I'll do whatever the team needs me to do," I said again, ashamed.

"I knew you would say that," Coach said again, and waved me out of the room.

In the NBA, there are a few set answers: "I take what the defense gives me." "I only want to win." "It's a team game." And so on. It's the brand we all have until we're big enough to have a brand of our own. I wanted to think I was big enough, but I knew any bigness was about being the first Asian American basketball star, not about the long, hard years of stardom that someone like Powerball! had earned. My role was to smile and say I was not overlooked—which was as close to a brand as the first Asian American basketball star could get.

I knew the image expected of me, down to the curve of my lips. I knew what I owed that image, my agent, my coach, my team, the NBA. I had to forget that every kid who grew up like me, like Sung, wishing to see an Asian American basketball star, was waiting for me to speak to them now.

As I dressed, I got a text from Carrie: Call me when you're done. Remember what you've accomplished.

I wore a suit to the postgame interview, having learned to bring clothes for TV. Coach sat on one side of me, and Powerball! on the other. It was the first time I sat in the middle. The mood was different from the last seven postgames. The reporters didn't joke with me, didn't ask what my story was. They had finished that story; they wanted to know what would happen next.

Coach said we couldn't wait to play together, Powerball! and me. We said we couldn't wait to play together. Powerball! said stop trying to get us to fight. I said, as a point guard, I would love to play with four Powerball!s: I could sit there and pass all day. Powerball! said get ready for a playoff run. The sea of reporters was as white as ever, much whiter than the players, though not as white as management. I felt myself leave my mind and float to the surface of my skin. Sung stood against the wall, at the end of the first row, and wrote down everything we said. He asked nothing. I thought: *Help me out, give me a question I can answer.*

Instead, as the interview wound down, Sung asked if I had seen a tweet from a famous boxer that what the Knicks really needed was size, and everyone knew Asians didn't have it.

I hadn't known about the tweet; now I did.

"You see the article comparing you to a Korean grocer in a Black neighborhood, Won?" Sung added.

I didn't understand what he was doing. He knew I had to seem grateful and optimistic; he knew the model. Asking these questions made it look like he was the real Asian American and I was a fake, a banana who cared only about himself. He was so different from the reporter who, two weeks earlier, had pushed Coach to promise he would start me, who had taken me out to dinner to celebrate.

I knew the history of Koreans in Black neighborhoods, of course; I had listened to salespeople insult Black folks in Korean. I knew how Koreans, forced out of white neighborhoods, took advantage of Black labor and Black customers. But to mention this now would be career suicide.

A few of Sung's colleagues side-eyed him, not expecting this attack, though maybe they didn't expect it because we were both Korean, not because Sung didn't seem like the sort of person.

"If millions of fans in Asia vote you into the All-Star Game," Sung asked, "will you give up your spot to someone who's played all season?"

Once I got away from the press, I drove my new car, a black Escalade, straight to the club the team liked. On the drive, I voice-texted Sung through the speakers. "What the fuck was that question mark," I yelled at the media console. "Off the record period."

I waited for my phone to buzz, then asked the car to read my messages. "I'm sorry," a flat male voice read. "But I'll go on the record if I have to."

I honked at a white guy who ran in front of me when we weren't even stopped in traffic.

"Hey, Siri," I yelled at the console. "Text Robert Sung, 'You fucking coward period.' "

Sung did not respond.

I started to feel nervous. "Hey, Siri," I yelled, "text Robert Sung, 'This is off the record period you got reporter integrity comma don't you question mark.' "

Sung did not respond.

I pulled off to the side of the street, or as close as I could get, and double-parked a white Civic.

The honking was immediate.

Carrie's text stared at me, but I was so pissed I brushed it aside. Literally.

This is off the record, I typed with my thumbs as the honks continued. I locked the doors. You're fucking shameless, I texted. You're the one who's going to ask me those questions, you asshole? You? You know I have to follow the fucking script.

Sung did not respond.

Off the record, I texted.

Sung did not respond.

Robert, I texted. Honk. Honk. This is off the record.

Finally, a text came back: Just say ur a team player. Nothing else. I drove on again, furious. At the next intersection, I read over the text once more.

Each time I stopped, I wondered about the tone, I got more and more pissed. Was he saying ignore him and do what I had to do? That was best-case scenario. Or was he angry that I followed the script in the first place? That was more like him: nothing if not a hypocrite. He was a man who made his career praising the man who had ended his career.

I yelled at the car, "Text Robert Sung, 'You're just jealous.'" But I canceled the text before it sent.

Words couldn't make me feel any better. I needed the kind of revenge that couldn't go on any record but the one among us.

9. SYMPATHY FROM MR. VENGEANCE

To be honest, I forgot about Carrie's text after that. The club was in the Meatpacking District, downstairs a regular dance club, upstairs a wide-open lounge with a view and its own doorman and bar. I had texted my new entourage to meet me in the lounge, and I found them huddled in a corner, a tiny Asian clique drinking on my tab. The group was me, Jin, Danny, Chow, and Handsome, who was the only one I knew from back when. The other three were clingers, but I had never had clingers before, so I liked them. I told them about Sung and my desire for revenge. I didn't even look for my special fan. I didn't want to see on her pretty face the devotion that Sung should have had for me.

I rounded up my boys to go on the attack. Just as we were leaving, Powerball! stepped in and power-moved me. He asked if I was ready to play together. He looked drunk, dangerous. Danny nearly knelt, he was so awestruck. Despite my glare to keep quiet, Danny said we were going to egg Robert Sung's apartment. He was the newest, one of Jin's friends, and I regretted my need to be adored.

Immediately Powerball! said he was in. Maybe he just felt bad for me after the postgame.

"What about your back?" Handsome asked. "You got to be a hundred percent, PB."

But it was impossible to contradict him. Not that he had anything to say about Asian America, he was simply in if he said he was in.

We rolled.

Handsome was DD—I had called him Handsome ever since we were kids, when the girl I liked said we were popular because I acted white and he was handsome, and sorry, she preferred looks. That left an impression on me, because weren't both of those things about looks? We were all in the same high school, but in reality, I was in a school within that school: college prep for kids who tested well or had money. That rejection was my come-to-Jesus moment. After Handsome took up with the girl I liked, I learned to see myself as someone different from how other people saw me. In the end, Handsome and me survived that girl. We survived many things, even the school within the school, even our town within a town, even me going East for college and him going nowhere.

In the back of the Escalade, Danny and Jin grilled Powerball! Chow played it cool. He chewed and snapped his gum with his mouth open. Handsome pulled up outside an Asian grocery, and Chow went in for the eggs. When he came back, he had two bags. A familiar smell came from the second. He snapped his gum with a stupid grin. Jin looked in the bag and slapped the back of Chow's head. The gum flew.

"What's the kimchi for, man?"

"It's symbolic, you know."

Handsome mouthed a laugh beside me.

"You're not even Korean, Chow."

"All Asians eat kimchi, you asshole."

Powerball! leaned forward and sniffed, then he held his nose and pulled from the champagne bottle. With his other hand, he pointed at the container, his eyebrows arching.

"You don't know kimchi?" Chow asked him, not unkindly.

"We're going to teach that reporter a lesson," Handsome said. "Not make his house a Korean taco."

"How you even live in New York, PB?" Chow said. "I mean, it's everywhere. No offense."

When we pulled up to a brownstone in Crown Heights, I felt grave, as if, instead of going to egg his house, we were going to murder him. A quaint brownstone wasn't what I expected. I realized I had pictured a house in LA, not a quarter of a building. I thought of my dad's small house, with the shabby blue paint job I did because he refused to pay housepainters and the city-mandated pretense of trees and him inside watching Sung grill me on national TV.

Luckily, Sung had a first-floor apartment. None of us had even considered that he might live higher up. There was something about him that matched a life on the ground. Each floor was split into two apartments, one on either side. Sung's was the right—we could tell from the numbers on the door. I handed out the eggs, then headed down the alley between his building and the next. When I reached the window, I heard yelling.

It was a woman's voice, high and abrasive. I hoped Ducky was letting him have it.

Powerball! pushed in beside me. I would have preferred Handsome, who had been with me the last time I egged a place, after my mom died. Suddenly I felt both much younger and much older than I was.

This was what happened: My mom had died of a stroke. She was only thirty-nine, with no risks in her medical history. It was like God blinked. One day, I was a twelve-year-old with no idea that I could lose her, and the next day, I was living some stranger's life. We had her cremated according to her will, but when we got to the funeral home, they handed us the wrong urn. At first, we thought they had sealed her inside this ornate metal thing she would have hated. But the urn turned out to be someone else's ashes, another Miyoung Lee.

That night, Handsome and I took all the eggs in our two fridges to the funeral home. I didn't notice my sisters following me. They let us throw one egg each before they stopped us.

Powerball! had to crouch down to see through the window, and I wondered how we looked to an outside observer, this huge Black guy creeping in an alley with five Asians. It dawned on me that there were two voices inside with Sung, not one. Both assumedly female. One accusing and the other accused. I couldn't make out the exact words. I cradled my eggs like grenades. When I raised one, Powerball! pushed my hand away, forcefully. I mean, dude almost threw me to the ground, and I thought about how a star is always a star, even in someone else's revenge. There was another window a few feet away, where Danny and Jin stood, eyes bugging, so I dug in between them.

It was two white women, one naked, while Sung, also naked, stood to the side. I could see part of the face of the dressed woman—Ducky—and her face was full of rage. Sung was cheating on her after all. She had caught him red-handed. She didn't seem surprised as much as proved right when she hadn't wanted to be right, as if she knew the other woman, whom I couldn't get a good look at. In my head, I urged the woman to turn just a little, but all I could see was a toned white ass, like it saw a daily workout. *Two white women,* I thought scornfully. I didn't like the suggestion forming in the back of my thoughts, that although Sung was clearly not enjoying himself, we should be jealous of his sex life. I didn't think I felt jealous. I glanced over at Powerball!, still resentful that he was in my spot, where he had a slightly better angle. He was as quiet as a turtle.

I wondered what was going through his mind. He looked completely different from how he acted on the court—scared and weak and small. He had tucked his arms and legs into his thoughts. He stared openly at the ass. He didn't seem aroused though; he seemed in disbelief, like the ass was a unicorn.

Chow made some stupid joke, and Handsome shushed him. My childhood friend wanted the same thing I wanted now—to get out of there.

I gestured to go back to the Escalade.

Jin left the kimchi outside the back windows. The eggs lay on the ground like unexploded bombs, duds. Days later, Sung would find the kimchi after a stink built up and he couldn't figure out what it was.

But Powerball! didn't leave the window. He crouched, making fists, then ducked as if someone had spotted him, and flattened his back against the wall. He shut his eyes. Then he did the last thing I expected: he cried, drunken, silent, ashamed. He already knew, or at least suspected, what we wouldn't know until later—that the other woman was his wife, Brit Young.

We left him there. I think, seeing our idol cry for the first time, we were trying to protect him. Not from what *he* saw, since it was too late for that, but from what we saw. He hated anyone to know he was human.

As soon as Handsome dropped me off at Carrie's apartment, I remembered her text.

10. CINDERELLA STORIES

The next morning, I made pancakes for breakfast, Carrie's favorite. I said casually that my phone had died. She said hers had too. It was a stalemate. She didn't mention the text. When she asked if I wanted to talk about the game, I said I had done everything I could. "That's right," she said. "If other people say different, that's on them, not you. You don't deserve that shit." I didn't tell her about almost egging Sung's apartment. I should have called her right away. Guiltily, I asked about her night. She had a lot going on then: Her sister had just been diagnosed with stomach cancer and they had watched the game from the hospital—with my newfound influence, I had gotten her sister into Sloan Kettering on short notice, so at least the Wonder had helped one other person in a material and significant way. Carrie said she was hopeful, the doctors seemed prepared for anything, but her sister knew it was bad.

Finally, she said, "I thought we were going to be together when we were together. Neither of us should have to tough things out alone."

After the news about her sister, what she said humbled me.

I *had* felt alone, and I had tried, on my own, not to feel alone.

"Okay?" she said.

"Okay."

"Then next time you'll do better. Let's forget your lies about the text I sent."

Over breakfast, I tried to do better. We talked about life in the face of death, hope in the face of fear. I mean it got heavy. I listened. Carrie said, lately, she believed even more in an afterlife because the worst thing would be if death was not a mystery but the end of mystery. She said she felt the most hope when the world turned out to be bigger than what it seemed. The Wonder, and K-drama, made her feel this way. Like her sister might suddenly and mysteriously heal.

I understood that she was giving me a chance to change. Maybe this was the most one person could ever give another. I was used to people who couldn't see beyond their own limitations putting those limitations on me.

In other words, we waited until after breakfast to check our phones. I had twenty-plus messages. Carrie's phone really had died. When she had enough charge to turn it on, she said she had a ton of messages too. "Look," she said. "They all say, 'Did you see the headline?' What headline?"

At the bottom of my notifications, there was a text from Robert Sung: Not my headline.

I started to feel concerned.

According to the time stamps, Sung had texted earliest. Whatever the headline was, he had wanted me to know it wasn't his before I saw it.

Carrie opened her laptop, and we recognized the headline immediately. It was splashed across the home page of ESPN: "The Great Wall Crumbles," with a photo of me with my hands on my hips, hanging my head.

"They couldn't even find something Korean to erase you with," Carrie said.

E-race, I thought.

I couldn't bring myself to laugh.

Even if it wasn't Sung's headline, it was his writing, his article. Carrie read it aloud. At first, she swore under her breath—"That asshole made you the model minority"—but soon she saw that if she kept cursing, she would have to curse me.

The article began with the typical Cinderella story, how I got my "chance" and "came out of nowhere," was "an overnight sensation," as if Coach was my fairy godmother. Then came my stats during the winning streak and the media frenzy and the questions about Powerball!'s return, followed by my stock responses: "I just want to win," "Powerball! gives us the best chance to win," "I'll do whatever the team needs from me." The part I dreaded came at the very end. In the final two paragraphs, Sung laid out the backlash: the boxer who had implied I had a small dick and the op-ed comparing me to a Korean grocer and the controversy over my possible inclusion in the All-Star Game (if fans from Asia ended up voting for me en masse, as they had done for other Asian, though not Asian American, stars).

My palms, instead of sweating, felt dry and puckered.

"Comments from Lee were requested to stay off the record," the article ended.

"What does that mean?" Carrie asked.

Sung hadn't printed my texts, at least. I wondered whether I should be grateful for that.

"What does it seem like?" I asked her.

"Are you kidding me?" But then she pursed her lips and squinted, reassessing. "Actually, I guess it seems like you got mad and didn't want everyone to know it."

"That's better than saying nothing, right?"

"Did you tell him off?" she asked. I could hear her thinking:

Or did you say you just wanted to win and would do whatever the team wants you to do?

Thankfully, I remembered what she had said about not toughing it out alone.

I showed her the texts.

My agent had already emailed twice that morning that I should keep my eyes on the prize, and the second time, as if I might not get it, had added, Note: the prize is money. Respect won't even feed a dog. I sent back a link to a designer dog food named Respect, just to troll him.

"Do you think Sung was trying to help me?" I asked Carrie.

The article had made me seem pissed but prudent, like I was a victim of racism who wouldn't play the race card. That might look best for me, at least with white people.

"You should go out there tomorrow and put up forty," she said. "Take every shot."

PART TWO
CARRIE

1. IT'S A CAKE!

For a while, there were these popular YouTube videos in which a person would present what looked like an everyday object—a bowl of fruit, a rice cooker, a Rubik's Cube—then slowly cut into the object until they had a slice. At that point, the person would lift out the slice and show that it was actually a cake, complete with layers and frosting.

On my favorite account, the creator was a tiny Asian mom who, each time she lifted out the slice, would shout with amazement, "It's a cake!" as if she hadn't known. Eventually, the objects became more impressive—a bouquet of flowers, a sneaker, a cup of coffee—until she made this one video in which the screen showed only her two hands and a knife, and then she picked up the knife with one hand and cut open the other. As usual, she shouted, "It's a cake!" with glee. I got to watching that video on repeat, especially late at night when I suffered from jet lag. Each time, the hand looked so real. "It's a cake!" I would say with her. It got to be a mantra, something I could say whenever life turned out to be more than it seemed. I would picture the woman chewing a slice of herself and moaning as if she were the most delicious thing in the world.

2. THEY SAID I MADE EVERYTHING A PRODUCTION

Around the same time I met Won, half a year before the Wonder, exciting things started to happen with my career. The production company I worked for in New York wanted to get ahead of the latest craze, which was Korean miniseries, or K-drama—and, being Korean, I got the job. The tokenizing would have normally upset me, but I had been hooked on K-drama since I was a kid. Me and my sister, K, whose name was Cassandra but who I had called K ever since I was a toddler (some amalgam of her first syllable and the other letter that sounds like *C*), had grown up watching K-drama with our mom. From the beginning, the plot twists had fascinated me. Maybe because I was the youngest, I never saw anything coming. Later, I learned the tropes. K and Mom would complain whenever I predicted what would happen. But I liked being right. A tight plot made me feel the kind of awe I was supposed to feel from religion: that whatever happened *had* to happen, that what was unlikely was a matter of perspective.

To be a minority in America is to guard what you love against other people's scorn. (For instance, I had stopped trying to convince people to try durian.) What I mean is, K-drama wasn't a craze; it was life. Finally, the life I knew was about to hit the mainstream.

After endless teleconferences with bigwigs in Seoul, my production company invested a lot of money in the project I recommended, and when the show was a go and was ready to shoot, I flew over, full of enthusiasm. I didn't have to adjust to the language or culture—or, for that matter, the drama—only the different hierarchy. For example, what I called a director, they called a PD, which was an abbreviation of "producer." What I called an executive producer (my title) they called the Korean word for "chief." They called the station executive the same word, which at first confused me. (I had to know these titles, which were how we referred to one another.) I didn't fit my team's expectations of a chief. The station chief never visited the set, while I tagged along on A-team shoots with the main PD and flew back and forth overseas, making calls from one country to the other. The whole staff eyed me warily.

At least, since I was the boss, criticism stayed behind my back. To my face, my team listened politely. I didn't mind them letting off steam on their own: a boss is there to be burned. The one thing I wanted was a woman PD. I made sure to find someone I clicked with. The PD was a quiet, forceful woman in her midthirties, short (to me), with long hair she never let down, sunken cheeks, and a jutting chin. Each time I saw her, she wore a different silicone bracelet, as if she had an inexhaustible supply of them. She maintained the aura of someone who knew your weakness and refrained from using it only because she didn't have to. It was her first drama after several successful variety shows, and I had wanted to work with her as soon as I heard her reputation for being extremely "lucky." It was what men said about me. It meant she got shit done without their help. That was the same in either country.

The only other person on the crew who seemed to like me was the PD's assistant, who would run up with coffee five times a day. He was the last true believer in Hollywood, angling for a connection. I got to like and expect his attention, especially as it was the only attention I got without asking. He was unnervingly handsome, with big eyes and a tiny head, and if he were taller, he would have fit the Korean ideal, but he was the same height as the PD. I was pretty sure he had a crush on her (I thought with a little envy).

The rest of the crew seemed to get from me the impression that American executives were tall, lazy, hungry women who had the time to visit the shoot and yet, when they did visit, always were the first to leave. Shoots in Korea often went twenty hours straight, with actors getting whatever sleep they could get between scenes or even going off for other business and returning. It was brutal capitalism. Shooting continuously lowered costs—when I tried to get more money for proper working hours, the PD insisted this wasn't done. We had to do it the Korean way, which was to make every won count. I settled for feeding everyone first thing in the morning, then early lunch, then early dinner, then once more after I left. A few times, I spotted actors on IVs and had to ask the PD to give them an American break in my American boss voice.

The drama was a romantic comedy called *For the Love of Your Future Self.* The male lead was a freakishly accurate fortune-teller who sees his gift as a curse. He doesn't want to know the future and tries to quit, but not telling fortunes makes him sick. He literally can't stop without feeling tortured by fate. Unlike in Hollywood, in Korea, plot happens because of who people are, not because of what they choose. They have to deal with the circumstances of their lives whether they cause those circumstances or not.

The female lead was a college student who can see ghosts, an ability that terrifies her throughout her childhood and makes her an outcast in college. She wants to get rid of her gift as much as the fortune-teller wants to get rid of his. Her greatest wish is to live like other people, to go to classes without fear that the next student who sits beside her will be dead. To survive, the woman closes her eyes to the world. She walks with her head down, staring at the sidewalk, never looking around her. In this way, fate brings the two leads together. Not watching where she is going, she walks straight into him.

The instant they touch, she sees the fortune-teller's gift/curse clearly. A ghost clings to his back—the ghost of a court seer killed by a king for foretelling an unlucky future. The woman has never encountered such an old and powerful ghost before. She hurries away, but too late. The ghost realizes she can see it, and it leaves the fortune-teller and attaches to the woman.

The fortune-teller is free; the woman who sees ghosts is doomed.

Just like any meeting between a man and a woman.

The PD laughed at this joke, which I made on the phone from Los Angeles. This was around the Lunar New Year, I think. I was trying to secure some media coverage and interest from American showrunners in remaking the drama in English, which was the next step toward my dream to make a Korean American Korean drama. The fortune-teller show had a good premise, so I had some serious interest from people with a lot of fucking money. The problem was they all wanted to cast white actors. I argued it wouldn't be following the rules. In K-drama, white people appear on-screen only to cause trouble or racism, or for an easy laugh, or as a representation of the corruption in the West. White people aren't characters; they're plot devices. As soon as they come on, we know they are there for their whiteness, which American stories pretend is never a factor. I told the PD all of this.

"Of course it should be made with aliens," she said, meaning white people. "We're making it right now with Koreans."

Suddenly I remembered this wasn't her battle. Strange how I could forget. "What does your bracelet say today?" I asked, to change the subject.

"'Monkey can't buy happiness,'" she said in English. "You should get Brad Pitt."

"He doesn't do TV shows."

"Then make them listen," she said. "Show them your power."

I had pitched the American pilot to start with the fortune-teller foretelling the entire season's events—a prophecy that might make it easier for an American audience to adjust to fate and circumstance as the driving engines of their lives, or at least of the characters' lives, instead of free will and agency—which proves I was willing to make some concessions. Race, however, is never a concession. It's exactly the kind of limit the show was about, the kind that white characters always seem to think they can overcome through heroic action, but which can only be faced and understood through love.

3. SEEING IS BELIEVING

I almost missed the game that started the Wonder—I was supposed to be on a plane to Korea, but I took a later flight to see Won play. I watched the win from Brit Young's seats behind the bench. Here is something you might not know about basketball, because I didn't know: Each player gets four tickets to a home game and two tickets to an away game. If players want more, they have to broker a trade. In New York, no one ever has a problem finding a friend who needs a ticket, so spares are rare. The best tickets go to team captains and to players with the most seniority, and the worst go to rookies and players with the least seniority. On the Knicks, Paul Burton got the best tickets, right behind the bench. Somehow, Won got the worst tickets, sixteen rows farther up, in a corner. I wasn't sure why, since he wasn't a rookie, he was in his third season in the league, but I also knew it was the same reason why he had the most expendable contract on the team.

At the beginning of February, when the Knicks were left with no other options, Won knew he was going to play. But he had only two tickets left. He'd already promised the other two to a friend on the opposing team who had grown up in the Bronx.

The way Won is, he refused to ask for those tickets back. He tried to gamble for more and ended up losing the two he had. I had to call Brit Young myself.

It wasn't easy to call her. Brit and I had a complicated fate. She had acted in the first movie I ever produced, an indie film about a small-town university professor who has an affair with a student, both women. The professor is a respected Jesuit theologist. No one's ever seen her with a date, so everyone assumes she's married to the church (also straight). Brit's character is her protégée, the only other woman among the theology faculty and the one person who discovers the affair. She's conflicted over what to do about it. She starts dreaming about her mentor—fantasizing, really. In her fantasies, she takes the place of the student. She, who thinks she is straight, kisses and touches her mentor. These fantasies terrify her, as if what she knows about her mentor takes over what she knows about herself.

I had done the film because of this battle between the mind and the heart. My family was super emotional, always crying and laughing and screaming while insisting on rationality. In college, my dad had barged into my NYU dorm and made a scene about how he would pull me out of school if I chose a film major. "Choose a practical major," he shouted, a line my friends and I would repeat all year ("I'm going to get drunk and kiss someone"—"Choose a practical major!"). But in Korea, my dad had been an engineer, and he had given that up to move to a strange country and marry my mom.

Why was it so difficult to get the mind and the heart on the same page? That was the film's theme. Some people (men) will have you believe the heart is the problem, fickle and deceptive, but only the mind is so easily swayed. For loyalty, you can't beat the heart.

Brit and I bonded over that theme. She was married to one

of the biggest superstars in the world, but according to the news, he cheated on her. She always looked weary on set. She was stunningly beautiful, tall and curvy, with perfectly cascading hair and perfectly chiseled cheekbones, yet there was a sharpness to her eyes and nose and mouth and attitude that said she was the wrong person to cross. We had cast her for this lurking quality. When she got into her role, she really seemed to be tearing apart from the inside. She seemed to be holding her contradictions together with all her might.

At that time, I worked for a smallish production company that three of my film school friends had started with money from their rich parents. One had left, and I had joined after that. We were all worried about stability—each of us, in a way, wanted to prove to our parents that we would be fine. My friends hadn't wanted to pursue a film about lesbian theology professors. It hadn't seemed lucrative. I insisted. To everyone's surprise, the film took off, especially on streaming. Our company became financially stable, and I got headhunted for a ton of money at a bigger company headed by a famous producer. The only person the film hurt was Brit. Her performance was so good it actually worked against her. She was typecast as both a whistleblower *and* a lesbian, a combination too much to overcome. Indeed, for years, men in the business would shake their heads and say, what a shame that Brit Young had wasted her talent, while they gave her no opportunities.

After the filming, Brit kept in touch, yet each time she was passed over for a role, it got harder for us to talk. I felt bad for her, and she hated pity more than anything. One of the last times we drank together, she opened up about her husband's infidelities. When I tried to hug her, she said, "It's all your fault. I shouldn't have done that film. Your mind-heart bullshit fucked my whole life."

The next time we spoke was when Won joined the Knicks. We acted as if that outburst had never happened.

At the game, I sat on one side of Brit's two youngest kids and she sat on the other side. The oldest stayed home and played video games. I apologized for taking his seat. "He doesn't care," Brit said. She rolled her eyes. "He's eleven. His dad isn't even playing." The seats were something else. You could smell the sweat, hear the sneakers squeak when players changed directions, see the secret elbows they threw when the refs looked the other way. Some players pinched. "Who's the Chinese kid?" I heard the opposing center say when Won came in, as if they hadn't practiced for him at all. When he hit his first shot, Brit turned and smiled at me over her kids' heads. I felt warm toward her again, like nothing had ever come between us. She did the same with his second shot, and his third. Then she stopped. Won had his way on court. The jumbotron found us, me and Brit on either side of her kids, and on that giant screen, I recognized her expression. It took her a second to realize she was on camera, and in that second, I was taken straight back to the set. A troubled line creased her forehead, and she squinted slightly and chewed the right side of her upper lip. I used to think of that gesture as not hers but her character's: conflicted about something, desperate and guilty and full of desire.

Once the camera left us, I followed Brit's eyes, out of curiosity. She didn't look toward her husband, on the bench, or toward any of the players—she looked directly at the press seats. Her teeth returned to her upper lip, and her head dipped slightly, a barely recognizable nod.

The only reporter I knew was Robert Sung, whom Won had more or less befriended, a strange-looking Korean with a big head and big ears and big shoulders, as if he wore invisible shoulder pads. I remembered Won telling me that Robert had been in love with Brit in high school. Our eyes met, and I smiled at him, expecting some sign that he was as excited as I was. Instead, he turned away and rubbed the back of his head, as though I had caught him doing something wrong.

I noted this, at the time, but I didn't have a chance to think about it. On the court, Won drove and scored, drove and scored, leading an impressive comeback. Something huge was happening, a legend being written right in front of us. There was a group suspension of disbelief—this collective sense of witnessing a miracle—with none of the skepticism or scrutiny that would come later. The crowd waited on Won's every shot, and each one that went in seemed to take us further from our old lives and into the future. How could I not have been thinking of K-drama?

Afterward, Won was interviewed for the first time on court. I couldn't even hear him. Fans chanted his name, drowning out the loudspeakers. He was a guy on the end of the bench who had turned in a game-winning performance, which in itself was thrilling, but throw in race and to have an Asian American player do that? The one Asian American player in the NBA? It was something no one had ever seen before.

No one left the arena—or no one but old people and Brit.

As Won talked to the on-court reporter, Brit gathered her kids and, before I could even ask her which exit to leave through, they made their way down the row. Everyone else stood and cheered. Brit stumbled on someone's foot and must have sworn, because her youngest yelled, "Mommy, don't say bad words!" loud enough for me to hear her from where I stood. Brit froze. She turned on the girl and, just as loudly—I'm sure only to be heard over the noise—shouted, "Mommy is not bad." Her daughter flinched. Brit took her hand and they kept going. At the end of the row, before she turned up the stairs, she seemed to glance over at the press seats once more. But my attention was back on the court, where Won waved and made a heart with his fingers.

After the game, I headed straight to the airport. By then, I had gotten so good at packing that I took only a carry-on. I had left a suitcase at the hotel in Seoul and a few outfits at a dry cleaner and some other things with a cousin on my dad's side of the family who always wanted to visit the set because he was a fan of the main actress.

When I took my seat on the plane, I felt too hyper to rest, so I paid the Wi-Fi fee and read every bit of coverage I could find online, which was not much yet since no one knew Won would keep playing his head off. Then my sister FaceTimed and said she had seen the game. She was full of hope. We talked for a while, and I reminisced about the game we used to play as children, which we had called "Romance." We would cover our dolls with a blanket or a sheet and make them whisper to each other, "Romance," "Romance." Since we shared a room, we played with our own bodies too; sometimes we would fall asleep under a blanket together, whispering, "Romance." The more we played the game, the more powerful the word became, the more mysterious and secret. Not that anything perverted was going on—it was just the power of shared language.

I said today I had felt a kind of romance with everyone in the arena.

K said we had grown out of that game. It was true that we had adapted "romance" to other purposes. K was barely a year older than me and we had a twin-like connection—if I had a stomachache, Mom or Dad would say, "Cassandra must be hungry," and five minutes later, K might walk in and ask for something to eat, which our parents thought was hilarious. "Romance" was K's word for what we felt. In third grade, I was sitting in class one day when my arm went completely numb. I shook it, thinking it was pins and needles, and sharp pain exploded. The teacher thought I was acting out for attention. When I got home, K's arm was in a cast. She had broken it on the jungle gym at the same time I had felt her pain. I stuck my pinky beneath the plaster and whispered, so that only she could hear, "Romance."

"Don't say it's like we're in a K-drama," K said now, on the phone.

"But it is like that!" I said. "What power do we wield versus fate?"

I fell asleep at maybe 4:00 a.m. New York time. A couple of hours later, another call woke me.

This time it was Ducky, who, from the time we first met, had reminded me of Ms. Frizzle from *The Magic School Bus,* frazzled and erratic and yet somehow teacherly. She and Robert Sung had taken Won to dinner after the game. When I saw her name on my phone, my first thought was that Won had been attacked by an anti-fan. I was still groggy and my mind full of drama. The call came via FaceTime audio—Ducky must have put some thought into how she could reach me on the plane.

But it was no emergency, she just wanted to chat. We had never chatted before. At first, I had no fucking idea what she was on about. Then, slowly, I put it together from what I had seen during the game and what Won had told me about Robert and Brit in high school.

Ducky asked how I knew Brit Young, and I told her about the film. All on her own, she offered the history of her husband's one-time crush. This was a test. I didn't respond, since I was an adult and other people's love lives were other people's love lives. Plus I was tired. What was so important that Ducky would call at what for her was probably dawn and for me was the middle of an overseas flight?

"Did Brit Young say anything about my husband last night?" Ducky asked. "Or me?"

"Ducky," I said, "are you okay?"

"Why did you go to the game with her?" she whined. "I saw you two looking at my husband."

I had to explain the whole ticket saga, how I had asked Brit to let me sit with her and her children. It seemed the only way to calm Ducky's suspicion that Brit and I were somehow in cahoots, though I didn't know why we would be. Ducky was clearly agitated.

"Do you know what your boyfriend said at dinner?" she asked.

I said, as she knew, I was currently thousands of feet above the ocean.

"He wanted to take my hubby to some secret club, to see some slut who likes him."

I sighed. "Okay," I said. "Just so you know, Won and I have an open relationship. Not that it's any of your business."

"Oh," Ducky said. "I didn't mean—forgive me."

She didn't mean to mean, I thought: it was just who she was. I felt for her. She wasn't a bad person. Once, she had told me that her mom wanted her to go to law school, and when Ducky married Robert Sung and started working at a day care, her mom had said, "What's with all these children? You even married one. You're like me: not a caretaker type," and predicted a divorce.

"I'm serious," Ducky said. "I'm sorry."

"It's not a big deal," I said.

"Really I am."

"I don't want to lose any sleep over it."

She kept apologizing until I had to comfort her. Finally, she said she believed me, which was a strange way to put it, as if my forgiveness was what needed to be believed. How did they do that, I wondered. How did white women always make the story about them?

I wanted to bottle that moment as the reason why I didn't want them in my remake.

4. BOYS CLUB

When I got to Seoul, the fortune-teller K-drama was in chaos. While I had been watching my boyfriend become a basketball star, the Seoul Metropolitan Police had arrested five male actors and singers and taken more in for questioning—including our second male lead. While I was reassuring Ducky, the news broke on the biggest scandal of the year. A group of famous men had shared hidden-camera videos of them having sex with women over a group thread on KakaoTalk, the Korean messaging app. Two actors had already confessed. Everyone on the production crew and in the station was trying to figure out exactly what the deal was with the actor in our drama, who was hiding out and refused to talk to anyone. In the drama, he played a singer who goes to the same college as the woman who sees ghosts and is secretly in love with her. He takes her out for dinner and listens to her talk about the fortune-teller. He shows up whenever she's in trouble on campus—in one scene, he notices her, huddled and shivering, and walks straight through an evil ghost to get to her, sending the spirit away. He fills the Daddy Long Legs role, offering the female lead support and not confessing his feelings for her because he doesn't want to burden her with his emotions.

He was a popular actor, and his fans insisted he had nothing to do with the sex ring and was questioned only because of his friendship with a singer involved. To me, the way he holed up sent a clear message. I wanted him killed immediately—on the show. The station chief didn't want to do anything without an arrest. We had to hold a meeting.

The main PD and the writer joined us, but the rest of the crew kept filming the episode as it stood. The station wouldn't lose money for anything. If money was what they cared about, I knew what I had to do. We sat all together, the three of us women: the PD, the writer, and me. I tried to tell the male executives that in America, we would fire the actor in a second, but either they knew I was lying or they didn't like the comparison. That comparison was the thing I hated most about Korea though—how much it could be like America.

"Let's wait until he releases a statement," the CEO said, looking at his phone.

I said waiting was losing viewers, and, as he knew, our viewers were mostly women, and, as he also knew, viewers equaled money, so waiting was losing money. I spoke to him man to man.

And yet his response was that I was being emotional.

I started out of my chair. The PD tugged at my hip; I hated that she would do that. I said my emotions were worth millions of dollars to the station, so they had better be fucking respected.

After the meeting, the PD was cool toward me. Her eyes said: "You threw up in my home and now you'll leave me to clean up the mess." I had restrained myself as much as possible. I understood that she had been put in an awkward position with her bosses, but I also understood that what put her in that awkward position was not really her relationship with me; it was that we were both women angry about a sex scandal.

The writer was pleased with me. Unlike the PD, her job wasn't tied to any particular station. She complimented me, which only frustrated the PD more—she seemed to be rubbing it in.

When we got back to the set, the writer stopped us. "Shit," she said. "We have a problem." She said we couldn't kill off the singer character because the woman who sees ghosts would still be able to see him.

She was right. It was so ridiculous that I couldn't help laughing. After a moment, the writer laughed too. Our dear PD looked like she was going to kill us both.

In the end, we made the Daddy Long Legs character a ghost that had possessed the singer's body. The nice one wasn't the living singer, it was the ghost inside him. In the next episode, the ghost got out of the body and became a character of his own, played by a new, hotter actor.

The reaction was split. Many fans hated this change. Others thanked the show for getting rid of the actor, who eventually was arrested and confessed with the rest of them.

The ratings took a short nosedive. What saved us was the Wonder. With his third win, Won's story made it to Korean TV, and when people found out that his girlfriend was producing the show, the ratings bounced back higher than ever.

5. CASSANDRA COMPLEX

At the end of that week's filming, K called and said to come back to New York. She had gone to the OB, thinking she was pregnant, and the doctor had sent her for a biopsy. She just got the results and hadn't told anyone except her husband. Their marriage was five months old. Her symptoms were dizziness, indigestion, vomiting. Yet she was not pregnant. She had metastatic stomach cancer.

It was night in Seoul, and I was half a planet away from her. My first thought was that I was dreaming. I was surprised to think such a cliché, but what K had said couldn't be happening. It was as if my work had taken over my life.

"Did you hear me?" K said on the phone. "I have fucking cancer."

"Cancer," I said.

She started to cry.

I kept her on the phone as I stuffed my carry-on and taxied to the airport and bought a ticket (no flights until morning) and paid a massage chair and almost nodded off waiting for sunrise. I told her about the latest events in the fortune-teller drama, I told her about childhood friends I stalked on Facebook, I told her about anything I could think of... the cake videos on YouTube, the ahjumma who ate her hand...She hardly responded, but she didn't hang up. I talked because she hated silence. She stopped crying. When I ran out of things to say, I brought up our make-believe game, the one we had talked about last time.

I said: "I didn't feel anything. Why didn't I feel any romance?"

"No more romance," K said finally. "Romance has left the body."

"Maybe it's just on vacation," I said.

She scoffed. "Don't blame me," she said. "You never even put out."

I could hear the pain as she laughed.

A week later, K was in for her first round of chemo, which would take three days and make her hair fall out and wrinkle her hands and hurt, her doctor warned, like a medieval torture device. (K liked this doctor who spoke frankly about the pain and put in her head the image of an iron maiden.) To prepare, the hospital had surgically installed an IV straight to K's heart. She had a little port on her skin, just below her collarbone, which she said made her feel like an android. Won had managed to get K into the second-best cancer hospital in the world, right on the Upper East Side, where they had urged her to start treatment as soon as possible.

I spent the full three days beside my sister. We watched on TV as Won and the Knicks won their seventh game in a row, the sixth with him as a starter. I grew more and more attracted to him, which concerned me. If even one other person likes your crush, they can seem hotter to you. The entire nation was hard for my boyfriend.

K was Won's number-two fan. She got super into his playing style, an aggressive game of high risk and high reward. Both she and I had played on our high school basketball team, though neither of us was any good. We were tall. What I liked most about the sport was the element of surprise. You have a goal in mind, a destination, but to reach it, you need to convince people you have a different goal. You head-fake, you pivot, you no-look pass, you step one way and cross back the other. Basketball and K-drama are both cakes.

"It's okay for other people to like your boyfriend," K said from her hospital bed. She rolled onto her side, pulling on the cords from the machine that pumped chemicals into her body.

"I know," I said. "But I'm having sex with him."

"I used to be like that," K said, "passionate. Now look where I am."

I didn't like the direction she was headed.

"Am I going to die?" she asked.

"This is only your first round of chemo."

"Fuck," she said. "This Wonder is the best I've ever felt about America, and I have cancer. What a con!"

I said, "You're totally hot for my boyfriend."

Beside me, K's husband, Fred, groaned. "Fuck, Carrie," he said. "Can't you stop with your stupid jokes? God. She's getting *chemo.* She has *cancer.*"

I had basically forgotten he was there. It was like doom had vomited out of his face. K cried. I tried not to blame him: he had his own feelings that needed to be nurtured and accepted. "We're all stressed out," I said. I couldn't help but add, "Usually I'm very funny."

Fred buried his head in his hands and apologized.

After K's opiates kicked in and she fell asleep, I thought again about what other people loved. For a long time, loving what other people *didn't* love had been my way of loving myself. Until now, I had never had a crush on a famous actor or athlete. But there was clearly an appeal to collective love. Loving someone—like living with the knowledge of your impending death—suspends disbelief. The more people who believe in something, the easier it is to believe in it. For those seven wins, everyone in New York had fucking float-walked, the sky was bluer, randos stripped off their shirts in the middle of winter to reveal Won's number on their chests. Even my mom was now a basketball fan, despite no interest when her own daughters had played.

I led Fred out into the hallway and I tried to tell him that what my sister wanted was this kind of suspension.

"You're keeping her from taking it seriously," Fred said.

I said no one took it more seriously than K—who could?

Fred went back into the room, retreating into his cave of literal meaning. I called the PD about our fantasy world. I wanted to keep believing. No matter how much the fortune-teller and the woman who sees ghosts try to avoid each other, fate brings them together again. The woman wants to figure out who the new ghost is so she can satisfy it and send it on to the afterlife, but the ghost refuses to speak with her. It's the scariest ghost she's ever met—even other ghosts are afraid of it. If it won't tell her what it wants, all she can do is give it back. Meanwhile, the fortune-teller, thinking he is free, finally manages to quit telling fortunes. With no experience or education, he decides to invest. He finds an investment manager who promises to triple his savings. Having always known his future, the fortune-teller doesn't realize he is being scammed. He loses his savings and has to go back to work. He has to get back his ghost.

The writer had worked hard on these scenarios, depicting the leads as lovers whose lacks are perfectly filled by each other. I had read somewhere that basketball, counterintuitively, is about the body catching up to the ball. The basic rule since netball is that both body and ball can't move at the same time. The dribble is a way to free the body. In basketball, the body is always trying to reunite with the ball.

"How do we get free?" I asked myself in the hospital.

I prayed for my sister to receive and give love.

6. EMERGENCY ROOM

The day after Won's first loss, I had the unreasonable hope and bad timing to pitch my company a basketball K-drama as my next project. I missed part of Paul Burton's return to the lineup to do so. My idea was a romance between an American journalist and a Korean basketball star, shot in both countries, a perfect setup for transitioning K-drama to America and for me to lead that transition. The journalist would expose the star for betting on a game, but once her article ended his career, she would find out that he had only made the bet to pay his sister's hospital bills. I had been thinking about what the PD said about showing everyone my power. Maybe my power was risking being American in Korea and Korean in America, like two parts adding up to more than a whole.

I pitched the show to the guy everyone in our Manhattan office not-so-secretly called Top Dog (emphasis on the *dog*), plus higher-ups in LA who teleconferenced in. Top Dog said my current K-drama hadn't ended and we should see how it rated first. Then he added, "A *Korean* drama with *Americans*? Do you hear how that sounds like you don't know what you're doing?" As usual, everyone agreed with him. After the LA people hung up, he said he had seen my boyfriend's last game, the loss, and it hadn't surprised him.

"I don't know what that has to do with my pitch," I said.

"Because you want to make a show about him, right? No one is going to be interested. This whole Wonder thing will blow over in a month, and the kid will be forgotten."

He waved me out of his office before I could even reply.

Afterward, I watched the rest of the game at a bar, feeling unfinished, unsatisfied. I wanted to revenge all over the place. To focus on the game, I had to put my vengeance on hold. I hoped Won would prove everyone, even Paul Burton, wrong.

What I saw was Won and Paul running into each other. There's only so much empty space on a court, and they didn't know how to share it. The paint seemed to shrink. Paul would make what would have been a brilliant cut if Won hadn't drawn the defense into the same spot. While Paul took on a double-team, Won would wait for a kick-out, then Paul would spin around one defender and look for someone who should have been streaking to the hoop in the hole he had opened. On the bench, they both looked frustrated. Luckily, they didn't go at each other on live TV.

In the last quarter, losing badly, Won finally went into fuck-it mode. It was clear, even from the most awkward camera angles, how he took over the huddle despite the eye from his coach. He pointed his teammates into position. He waved away screens. And it nearly worked. The Knicks came back, but still lost. Won scored ten points in the last quarter. Paul scored ten points in the last quarter. Yet most of a game of cock-wagging and twelve minutes of teamwork does not a victory make.

The unfinished feeling came back. Won wasn't responsible for my problems with my company though. Top Dog didn't hate me because he hated Won; he was just racist. This time, instead of anger, I felt worry for both of us. In the fortune-teller drama, worry is a sign of love. The more worried the fortune-teller feels about the woman who sees ghosts, the more obvious it is that he has feelings for her. At first, he pushes her away, afraid to take back his ghost. But she needs his help. She explains her ability and describes the ghost he was carrying without knowing it. They spend more time together and learn about each other's lives. He sees how hard life is for her. Eventually, he becomes so worried about her that he would rather take back his ghost than see her suffer from it.

When my sister called, I was imagining ways to kill my boss, poisons that leave no trace. K had been rushed to the ER with a fever. I got the first Lyft I could. In the car, my worry seemed suddenly useless, unable to save anyone, merely a trick my mind played to make me feel like I was doing something by *feeling* something.

At the ER, however, K was fine, salty even. She said she hadn't wanted to go there, Fred had made her. "My immune system is so fucked, you know, Carrie, that other people's sickness could kill me quicker than my own. What am I even doing in this death trap?"

Eventually, a nurse entered, and we anticipated a verdict, a sentencing. It didn't come. Relieved, K confessed that the uncertainty was the worst of all, not knowing what was possible and what wasn't.

7. MAKING OUT

Finally, after the chemo and the failed pitch and the ER, I got back to Seoul. It was a Monday; I had missed a week's worth of shoots. The PD was prepping for the first-kiss scene, in which the lovers finally stop running from their feelings. The fortune-teller has his ghost back, but this means the woman who sees ghosts is afraid to go to him, afraid the ghost will return to her. Though now, at least, she understands him. She cares for him. She understands his worry for her by understanding her worry for him. Finally, that worry (that love) gets the best of her, and she can't stay away. As the lovers' lips meet, the ghost indeed releases the fortune-teller to jump back to the woman—yet this time, it can't attach to her. It can't get ahold of either of them. This is the power of a K-drama kiss. The power to put fate on a different course.

The actors prepared for that kiss now, freshening their breath. The PD grumbled about how I came and went whenever I pleased, not caring what she dealt with while I was gone. What *she* dealt with. It was personal for her. She was still afraid that I had rattled her bosses' cages, that they would take it out on her at some point. I wanted her to feel free to tell off anyone she wanted to. I wanted to hug her.

"The ratings fell again after your boyfriend's losses," she said.

"I missed you too," I said genuinely.

"You look *happy,*" she said, as if "happy" meant covered in shit. It was how disdainfully she said it that made me believe her. I hadn't thought of myself as happy. I had thought of myself as incredibly stressed out, dejected, overworked.

"I will be happy," I said.

"Will be?"

With the Wonder over, maybe I needed K-drama, more than ever, to remind me that anything was possible.

"My sister has cancer," I said. "What's wrong with trying to be happy?"

The PD crossed her arms. Her eyebrows went up like *Hello, look where we are.*

I didn't get it.

Her bracelet for the day read, "OTL," which was an emoticon of a stick figure despairing—or praying. "Don't you watch melodrama all the time?" she asked. "Happiness means unhappiness is coming."

I took her coffee and dumped it on the ground. "There," I said. "Unhappiness."

Suddenly I felt ashamed.

The PD raised a hand to stop her assistant from cleaning up the mess. I picked up the cup myself, careful not to stain my clothes. I felt jealous, though I didn't know why or which of them I was jealous of. My heart spun, confused.

When the actors were ready and everything was set, the marks and beats agreed upon, the PD called action. The actors moved toward each other extremely slowly. On the PD's screen, it looked like slow motion, but they were doing it manually, extending an instant into a minute of desire. Each centimeter really did make my heart flutter. Since K-dramas rarely show sex, a kiss has to carry the thrill of a sex scene.

The PD made them kiss over and over. Between takes, both leads moistened their lips. They seemed flustered, embarrassed. When the cameras rolled, they went back to it. Finally, the PD pulled my arm until I was right next to her. "Look," she said, and I saw what bothered her. Up close, the kiss looked far too sexy, too knowing. I felt turned on. I felt extremely conscious of how close I stood to the PD, of the intimacy of her hand on my elbow.

"They're fucking," the PD whispered to me. She meant in real life.

It was a cake!

"Let's try it again," she shouted.

Again.

Again.

But they couldn't go back in time, only forward. Ahead lay less curiosity, not more. I said maybe they should pretend they were kissing someone else entirely. The PD said that was what they were doing, it was called acting. She cackled. When her assistant appeared with a new cup of coffee, only one, he passed it straight to her before I could reach for it. My happiness wouldn't last.

8. KARAOKE

That night, I took the production staff out for barbecue and drinks and noraebang. Usually, teams waited until after a series ended to do this kind of outing; the weeks of shooting are intense and sleep becomes rare/precious—but some anxiety was pushing me. I paid personally, not with company money. As I went over the day's events, I wondered what was bothering me so much and why I couldn't let it go. All that came to me was the PD's face when she stopped her assistant from picking up the cup I'd spilled. I felt like I had to reassert my place on the team. For some reason, I was reminded of a panel I did on Asian American representation, where the one male panelist told the audience to see every Asian American film that comes out, see it twice or three times, because Hollywood listens to money. I tried to get across the irresponsibility of people like us, paid by the industry, telling others to spend their hard-earned cash if they wanted change. The guy sneered with such derision, and said *some of us* needed any role they could get, as if I was some elitist out of touch with society.

As the staff outing went on, the PD grew visibly upset. Her knees bounced. Seeing that, I felt justified for taking everyone out, though I didn't know why. It wasn't like any of them could refuse me. I was their superior. And many of them wanted to go out every night and only didn't because they knew they shouldn't. It was 3:00 a.m. when we started singing, and shooting would resume at five. There would be no sleep and many hangovers.

In the singing room, I ordered drinks and poured soju for the PD, trying to bring down her guard. The crew danced and sang. They knew an impressive amount of early-aughts choreography. The PD kept touching her hair, which made her seem younger than she was. She acted like she no longer knew who I was, like I could be anyone at all. Her uncertainty made me realize that I was showing off my power, but also that my power was no more real than the kiss scene. I wanted to do something to test it, like kiss the PD in slow motion. Did that mean power turned me on? Or wonder?

When the PD was drunk but not too drunk to remember, I told her about my basketball idea and asked her to continue working with me. It had to be her, as otherwise the show wouldn't mean anything. I asked her to do it even if we had to shoot on the sly, maybe dip into the company's coffers before they technically okayed it, or raise money from outside investors, or get another production company involved. I told her what I had so far, rethinking it as I talked: American journalist finds out Korean basketball star gambled on a big game; her exposé gets the star canceled; the star follows her around trying to defend himself in person (so they hate each other but are always around each other); then the journalist finds out that the money actually saved someone—a sick girl, an orphan—and feels guilty about her exposé, and that guilt leads to sympathy, which leads to romance, etc.

I talked and talked. I didn't know what else to do. Her assistant attempted the high notes in "Tears" and squeaked. Either the room spun or the lights spun—I couldn't tell which. I wasn't sure anyone was listening to me. Finally, someone cut "Tears" short and the PD's song choice popped up next. She waved one of the mics in my face. In my haze, I recognized this as a challenge, but I didn't know what that challenge was or why she was making it. Everyone who was left looked to me. What could I do? The song was far too slow and depressing for room karaoke, and the PD sang it beautifully, in a low, mournful tone that killed the mood.

I walked out to the lobby where the front desk ahjumma sat, and I asked her to turn off our music and end our time. The request confused her. She said we still had thirteen minutes left on the hour. I had to repeat myself several times. I almost shouted at her, an innocent person. My stomach hurt. The PD had turned my sincerity into an overwrought love song. She had mocked me and she had mocked the melodrama that was our work and our lives. My sister was dying, and that fact meant nothing could be too overindulgent or exaggerated. Nothing could make loving a dying person more melodramatic than it was.

9. MANNERS MAKE THE MAN

I must have blacked out, since the next thing I knew, I was sitting in the PD's assistant's car. I understood that he was driving me home. I didn't recall how this had come about, but it was clear that we were headed to the hotel and that someone had asked him to take me, either the PD or myself. He was very uptight about the task, as he was mortifyingly sober. He either hadn't drunk enough or had an intolerable tolerance. My phone buzzed with a text from Won, answering a text I must have sent him. His said: It's just 2 Ls. Mine said: You must be pisser? Sorry I had to letup. Lift. Who knew whether he got what I wanted to say to him.

I swore, and the assistant seemed surprised. "You know English curse words?" I asked in English.

"Yes," he said, giving the word two syllables.

"Good, because I'm too tired to curse in Korean. What time is it?"

It was 4:30. The shoot was about to start. The crew was on its way to the location, and soon the actors called for the earliest shots would show up and wonder why the crew was drunk and why the shoot had to be so early then. I would have felt bad for the PD, since I was the one responsible, but the sense of being humiliated and rejected by her lingered.

"Drive me to the fucking shit," I said. "I mean shoot."

He didn't respond. I said it again, in Korean this time.

"I'm not supposed to do that," he said too informally.

I was shocked. It was a serious breach, to use banmal with his elder and superior, as if he were no longer an assistant who ran errands on set but someone able to boss me. Maybe he thought he could do it because he was sober and I was drunk. Because he was a man and I was a woman. Because he was Korean and I was American. Because we were alone. If anyone else on the crew had heard him, he wouldn't have been able to show his face.

"Did the PD tell you to drive me home?" I asked in Korean.

He nodded.

Maybe he believed she could protect him.

Again, I pictured the PD stopping him from picking up the spilled cup.

"You're not going to take me to the set, then?" I said.

He didn't answer.

"Look," I said. "I'm your boss. Hers too. Even when I'm drunk and embarrassing. Do you understand?"

He glued his eyes to the road.

"Do you understand?" I repeated.

Finally, he said, "Yes, ma'am," in English.

When we got to my hotel, I made him walk me to my room. I think that "ma'am" was why I slept with him. I slept with him because there was still a language in which I dominated—he had broken the rules in Korean, so all he had left was English. I slept with him because he thought he was the PD's person, not mine.

He could barely look me in the eye afterward.

Later that morning, on the way to the airport, I called the PD and told her I had to head back to New York already. In the background, someone vomited. An actor shouted. Someone scolded the PD's assistant for being late. I could picture the chaos. The PD must have lost some authority after all. Everyone would know she had told her assistant to drive me home. He was probably still in his outfit from the day before. On the phone, I took my time. I said, "I guess I'll just keep coming and going whenever I please."

The PD laughed in a high-pitched, performative aegyo, the kind grown women do to seem submissive to their oppas. "Okay, Carrie," she said, not calling me "Chief" but using my English name. A shiver of yearning shot through me, and I pulled the phone away as if it had electrocuted me. From that distance, I told the PD to get it together and not overstep, and I hung up before she could laugh again in that keening, girlish tone.

10. A BRIEF TREATISE ON THE BODY

Maybe it takes a woman to see that this story is about the body. When K got cancer, when Won became a superstar, when I tried to bring K-drama to America, our bodies were exposed. I don't mean naked. Even naked, most people do everything they can to avoid exposure. I mean the limits of the body becoming the limits of the self. A cancer patient is never allowed to be anything but a cancer patient—that was what K hated the most. If I had done all the Asian American films I had wanted to do, I wouldn't have been allowed to do anything else. Bringing K-drama to America now would mean the Wonder wasn't just temporary. It would mean we had actually changed how our bodies are seen. What I'm saying is, I didn't want K to be defined by her disease, or Won by a "frame of reference," or me by a set of acceptable stereotypes, anymore—I didn't want to be classified, the way the adoption industry (my mom had told me) classified her and other children of color as "special needs" just because they weren't white.

If that's not clear, maybe a friend of mine who left the film industry to become a women's health lobbyist said it best: I had told her about my mom's frustration whenever someone co-opts adoption for one cause or another—the antichoice movement, for example. My friend replied that what scares those fuckers is the idea of other people's bodies being as free as their own. Nothing, she said, horrifies them more than their own bodies. This explains why certain people hate disabled folks and undocumented folks and trans folks, and so on. Though also why there are always people who will turn their back on a community that tries to love them.

II. FANDOM

The All-Star Game that year was at the very end of February. The Knicks had one last home game before the break. I took Ducky. I hadn't seen her since the beginning of the Wonder, and I worried. It took a while to get her to talk, which wasn't like her. On the court, Won and Paul still got in each other's way. On one play, they literally ran into each other and fell together to the floor. You could hear the collective sigh of grief. It was like we were watching two games at once: the actual game and the game that could have been if the Wonder never ended.

To distract from the court, I told Ducky about the fortune-teller show. By the halfway point of a K-drama, I explained, the couple knows they're in love, so the conflict in their relationship has to shift from a battle with their feelings to a battle over the acceptability of their feelings. In many cases, the show returns to a problem it has saved from the couple's pasts. One of my favorite examples is a romance between a reporter's daughter and the orphan her family takes in. They don't know how he was orphaned, and he doesn't say. His secret is that his parents were accused of a terrible crime and committed suicide. He knows that they are innocent, but he can't prove it. Halfway through the show, after the kids grow up and become lovers, the girl finally learns what happened to the boy's family: a reporter accused his parents on national TV, cornering them. That reporter was none other than the girl's mother.

In the fortune-teller drama, as in many romantic K-dramas, the first kiss happens right at the halfway point. The conflict that follows comes from the fortune-teller's ghost. After the kiss, the fortune-teller and the woman who sees ghosts think they are finally free to love each other. The ghost has other plans. It wants to know why the woman can see ghosts in the first place. What it finds out is that the woman is the descendant of a murderous king who killed his fortune-teller for predicting misfortune... and, you guessed it, the ghost is the spirit of that very fortune-teller. The ghost is the one who cursed the king's entire bloodline to eternally see the dead—so that they would see who was taking revenge on them. Having found the king's last living descendant, the ghost plans its ultimate vengeance: to possess the woman's body and make her kill the fortune-teller she loves with her own hands.

Overblown or not, it's the perfect twist. The ghost, in a way, ends up responsible both for bringing the couple together and for their biggest challenge. Even if the couple comes out alive, they have to confront the fact that their relationship nearly killed them.

This entire idea started as a joke: *What else is a relationship that almost kills you, if not love?*

Ducky didn't like this twist. In fact, she hated it so much that tears welled. I knew I had brought up a love relationship while her husband was cheating on her with someone else's wife, but I hadn't expected her reaction to go so far.

It turned out she was streaming the show illegally. She was very attached to the characters. *Very* attached. She had her own pet theories. I hadn't realized. She wanted to know why I would ruin *her* characters' lives. "Why can't you just let those poor kids be happy?"

When I asked what was really going on, why she was really so upset, it all came pouring out.

Ducky had caught Brit Young fucking her husband. She had gone home on a night she was supposed to spend at her mom's, and as if in a film, a trail of discarded clothing led to her bedroom door. She gathered every single piece and threw them all in the trash with her balled-up tampons and the cat's used litter, before she even interrupted them. Then she screamed as they stood there covering their crotches.

Ever since then, Ducky said, she couldn't stop destroying stuff. She barely realized she was doing it. She would look down and see that she had smashed the watch her husband always wore with a hammer.

It surprised me that she had this in her.

"The worst part," Ducky said, "was his excuse. He said—get this—although he loved and married me, he never stopped loving her. Can you believe that? *Although,* he said. I'm *although.*"

She was thinking about buying a gun.

In the stands, I hugged her and whispered not to cry or the camera would catch us. She came back to her point with stubborn resolve. In this most difficult time of her life, she said, did I have to go and make her characters, who love each other, attack each other? Why, she said, should the past even matter, especially if it isn't *their* pasts but something that happened before they were born?

She fixated on this idea that past attachments shouldn't stop a couple from loving each other now.

I held her hand and sympathized with her, in the Garden hushed with grief. I pictured her with a gun. Not a comforting image.

She was losing her innocence now, at twenty-eight. Only a white woman could hold on to her innocence for so long. And yet she really did love Robert. She simply wanted love to be faithful to the ideal she grew up with: princes and princesses and nonconsensual kisses that wake girls into women. It wasn't the K-drama ideal, but she was no less serious about it. She loved Robert so much that she would destroy every last piece of their life together, if that was what it took to make him want to protect it.

After the game, I called Brit Young. One of my high school friends had jumped off a building, and we had seen the signs for weeks, the desire to destroy, and the withdrawal, followed by a manic joy just before she did it. She had killed herself because one of the teachers had been sleeping with her and stopped. It was a giant scandal, but the teacher got out of prison after a couple of years. My friend was dead. I had known Brit far longer, and far better, than Ducky—yet Brit was the one crossing relationship lines. I knew that shouldn't matter (there I was, sleeping with the PD's assistant) but it did.

Brit had no problem telling me about Robert. She was completely aboveboard, for someone fucking someone below board. It was as if the Brit I knew from before, impassioned and eager to share that passion, was back. She said she was going to divorce Paul and marry Robert.

"How long have you been together?" I asked.

"Like a month," Brit said.

"A month?"

"I know what everyone will think," Brit said, not defensively, just matter-of-factly. "But he's loved me for fifteen years and that's exactly what I want now. I want someone devoted to me. I want to mean more than a sport."

I remembered on the set how she had sent flowers to herself

after the story broke that her husband was cheating on her. Robert was nothing if not a devotee.

"And you loved him too?" I asked.

"We're so stupid about our own feelings, aren't we?" Brit said. "Our feelings are pretty smart though."

Our feelings are pretty smart would become another maxim to me. I texted Won that I wanted to talk to him before I went back to Korea this time. If I knew anything about the episodic progression of love, something was going to change.

PART THREE
K-DRAMA
For the Love of Your Future Self

A PRIMER

K-drama, or Korean drama, is a genre of Korean TV. A typical K-drama airs twice a week in hour-long episodes for two to three months and completes its arc in a single season. A show usually lasts sixteen or twenty episodes. K-drama itself is split into contemporary and historical drama (called sageuk) and then into romance, thriller, etc. A contemporary drama is likely to revolve around a love story with two main leads and two second leads. A sageuk likely revolves around political intrigue. Traditionally, episodes are written and shot as the show airs. Before digital recordings, an assistant director literally hand-delivered a physical tape to the broadcasting station, sometimes minutes before the episode began. Very few K-dramas are shot like films, entirely before their release, and yet, unlike American shows, a K-drama is filmlike in that it is a unified whole, like a sixteen-hour movie, often with a single writer and director. Ninety percent or so of the writers are female. Most directors are male. When a K-drama succeeds, it can command double-digit ratings, and K-dramas that reach forty percent of viewers are called National Dramas, because of the shared experience.

Popular tropes in K-drama include body-swapping, gender-bending, ghosts, characters from folktales, temporary amnesia, sudden cancer, car accidents, contract relationships, Cinderella stories, Candys, Daddy Long Legs, assholes with a heart of gold, reincarnations, mistaken identity, enemies to lovers, birth secrets, last-minute sea changes, etc. Any viewer has favorite and least favorite tropes, but for the show's purposes, tropes are accepted ways to force the main leads together and/or apart. The following is the story of one such show, *For the Love of Your Future Self,* about a fortune-teller and a woman who sees ghosts.

I. THE WOMAN WHO SEES GHOSTS

Once upon a time in dramaland, there lived a young woman, Koo Mirae, who was particularly sensitive to the dead. Though at first the dead seemed like fingerprints on the photograph of her perception, Mirae gradually grew able to see them. This ability was a family inheritance. It was said that Mirae's grandmother had died because she failed to keep a promise to a ghost, and it took revenge. After her grandmother's death, her father couldn't take the ghosts anymore and left. Mirae had to deal with her ability on her own. (It is useful in K-drama for a character to make good on not only her own past but her family's.) Mirae's mother hated any mention of ghosts and refused to believe they existed, though most of the townspeople accepted ghosts as an unseen force among them.

In school, Mirae was feared and therefore bullied, and she hid her gift as best she could. In K-drama, a gift often seems at first to be a curse, which is a trope about learning to take responsibility. Mirae wished someone on her father's side was around to advise her. Her mother pushed her to study and eventually sent her to Seoul for university. To help pay her fees, Mirae took a series of part-time jobs, which meant she was always on the defensive against any new ghosts. She carried salt and talismans and never talked to anyone until she had verified that they were alive. She never looked at anything or anyone for too long. If the ghosts didn't know she could see them, they would treat her like anyone else. Only when she met their eyes did they come to her with their longing or resentment. They had tasks to complete or people to watch over or vengeances to carry out, and until then, they couldn't let go of their desire for a body.

In short, Mirae was able to move through the world by trying not to be a part of it. She kept her eyes on the ground, avoiding the dead and the living equally. She lived in neither world—she lived in a world of one. As long as she didn't notice it there, she could step straight through a ghost as everyone else did, with only a chill on the back of her neck. If she ran into someone living, she apologized and rushed away. It was easier to flee people's anger, she had come to believe, than their fear. She didn't realize how lonely she was.

It was while walking with her head down and shoulders hunched, being there without being there, that Mirae ran into her fate. She crashed right into the last thing she ever expected: someone else who was not fully in the world of the living or fully in the world of the dead.

2. THE FORTUNE-TELLER

Once upon a time in dramaland, there lived a fortune-teller, Song Hwaeen, who had such uncanny powers that people waited for months to see him. He had been telling fortunes since he was nine and had predicted the exact date and reason for Park Geun-hye's impeachment. It was said that he had tried to quit telling fortunes several times and nearly gone mad. He couldn't survive as a normal person. Indeed, living with his power, he had become a very particular young man. He followed a strict routine—a common starting point in K-dramas in which a control freak learns through loving someone else how to be kind to himself. Each morning after breakfast, Hwaeen prayed for three hours in a temple at the top of the nearest hill. He prayed to be freed from his gift. After praying, he ate lunch with the monks, who were vegetarians. After lunch, he descended the hill and, for four hours, met clients in a local coffee shop, until he left for dinner. He saw people in the order they contacted him and never took money in exchange for cutting in line. For dinner, he took the subway an hour away to his brother's barbecue restaurant, which was in another district of Seoul. At the restaurant, no one knew about his gift except his brother. His brother welcomed the daily visit as long as Hwaeen didn't tell anyone's future. When Hwaeen was nine, the first prediction he ever made was that their mother should avoid ice, and though she was careful, she slipped on stairs and fractured her spine, leaving her paraplegic.

His family had forgiven him for his warning (in fact, his mother never blamed him; she said it was because she was careful that she had lived at all) but Hwaeen never forgave himself. He believed he had cursed himself by telling that first fortune. That it was the reason why he couldn't stop. Why he knew only other people's futures and never his own. A personal torment is a good way to make a male lead more sympathetic.

On the day Hwaeen and Mirae met, he had come out of the subway and was waiting for the crosswalk light to change. His thoughts were on the fact that the train had run thirty-six seconds slower that day. The moment the light turned green and he lifted one foot to cross, a woman not looking where she was going slammed into him. Just before he hit the ground, he had the strange sensation that he was free of something, that all the effort he constantly put into ignoring the future was suddenly unnecessary and he had the energy to do anything, absolutely anything, else.

The woman, Mirae, bowed in apology and tried to rush on, but as Hwaeen had seen men do in K-dramas (though he had never done so himself, being a gentleman and also afraid of chaotic emotion) he caught her wrist. "Don't go," he said, looking up from the ground, unable to think of anything else to say. "Have coffee with me."

She gaped at his back as if he was carrying a child. She looked so shocked—or scared?—that he immediately released her.

"Sorry," he said, ashamed. "You don't know me. But—"

She was already racing off.

The sensation of freedom, however, remained. For the first time since he was nine, Hwaeen felt light and unburdened of the future.

3. TO GIVE UP THE GHOST

The ghost had gone with Mirae. Had clung to her back, actually, the way it had clung to the fortune-teller's back. At first, Mirae was sure only of some added burden, a feeling that she knew things she shouldn't know, that if she looked at anybody on the street long enough, she would see their most private lives. It was a maddening feeling. The closest thing she could relate it to was a time in childhood when her favorite cousin had chicken pox and Mirae wasn't allowed to go to her, because to do so would upset not only their parents but her cousin, who didn't want Mirae, younger and weaker, to catch sick. Or there was the time when Mirae wanted to announce to her entire high school that she finally had a boyfriend, but her boyfriend said that if she told anyone, he would dump her, and the ghosts taunted her about this every night until he dumped her anyway.

After rejecting the fortune-teller, she ran home to the tiny one-room she rented and got out her hand mirror—and there it was, its legs around her waist and its hands over her temples. "Please," she said, calling the ghost "mother" as if they were close neighbors, "don't come to me." But it was too late.

The ghost was a woman in her late thirties wearing an old-fashioned hanbok, pale with death's particular subtraction, face small and bony. It didn't exactly look evil. It looked desperate. Most ghosts were. Whatever they wanted, they wanted it so much that they had given up eternal peace.

"Please," Mirae said again, but the ghost seemed to press harder on her head. Suddenly Mirae could feel the presence of the couple in the next apartment over. They fought, their voices low and fists drawn. She hadn't known who was over there. Now she would forever know that on the other side of her wall, an unhappy couple beat each other up but didn't want their neighbors to know about their unhappiness.

She shut her eyes and screamed that she would call the police, and the fight seemed to end. Still the ghost pressed harder. Mirae shuddered with knowledge. More than their current pain, Mirae could feel all of the pain coming to them: their bad fate together and the way they would live out the same fight over and over again, unable to choose any differently. She felt their certainty that they were in control and the equal certainty that control was precisely the cycle they were trapped in. In the end, it was this certainty—that they could not escape who they were to each other—that sank Mirae to her knees. She dropped the mirror, unable to look at the ghost anymore, and fainted.

In most K-dramas, fainting presents the chance to see who will take care of the fainter. Add the second male lead, a Daddy Long Legs type who supports Mirae without ever winning her heart. Or add the second female lead, Mirae's only friend, who is about to become her love rival. The point is that when Mirae woke, her knowledge of the future was still there, fogging the rest of her thoughts, nearly debilitating. She reached for the mirror but thought better of it. How had the man she bumped into handled this feeling, when even she, so used to ghosts, could not? She had only one move: to find him and convince him to take his ghost back. She had made a mistake earlier, thinking he was asking her out—her heart had fluttered to hear what it had never heard before—when he must have wanted her help. She needed his help now, for his problem had become hers.

In this way, little by little, sharing their problem would become love. K-drama fates two people together who would otherwise convince themselves they should be apart.

4. UP AND DOWN

To put it simply: exchanging the ghost affected them in opposite ways.

Hwaeen became no more prophetic than the typical street psychic and promptly closed shop. He was once again Hwaeen and no longer the Fortune-Teller Who Can't Quit. Everything seemed to smell and sound and taste better. Flowers smelled more flowery, traffic sounded more human, ice cream tasted like he had never really had ice cream before. Because of his adherence to routine, he had plenty of savings for a while, maybe years. He could start a whole new life.

Mirae was even more despondent than ever. All her coping mechanisms failed. She avoided mirrors and windows and glass or metal of any kind, but even when she didn't see the fortune-teller's ghost on her back, it forced her to see the future. It was worse than being possessed, which had happened to her twice before. Her father had left her a talisman that kept ghosts from touching her. When she carried the talisman, the fortune-teller's ghost hovered behind her, waiting for her to put the talisman down—and this small distance eased the overwhelming voices, like stepping just outside a crowded room, but they didn't go away. She slept with the talisman in her fist. At work, she slipped it into her bra strap.

In her limited free time, she would walk by the subway stop where she had crashed into the man. She was sorry to want to give back the ghost, but her life was already difficult. Other ghosts hovered around her constantly now because they could see the fortune-teller's ghost. She overheard entire ghost conversations she wished she could forget. Sometimes they would talk about her. As word spread among the ghosts, more and more approached her with their notes and gifts and anger and evil intentions. The only good thing about carrying the fortune-teller's ghost was that none of the other ghosts would dare upset it, though this fact also worried Mirae the most.

Only a week passed before Hwaeen returned to his routine. He needed the familiar rounds. Instead of praying to be free of his gift, he went to the temple to thank the gods for freeing him. Instead of working at the coffee shop, he sat and read. It almost made him happy to inform the people who asked for fortunes that he could no longer predict a thing. His brother was amazed by the change in Hwaeen and kept asking what it was. His mother called and said, "You're free of it, aren't you?"

"I didn't even know you would call," Hwaeen said happily.

"You always knew? Then why was your phone turned off so often?"

She had caught him; he was overjoyed at being caught.

He was not overjoyed to find the woman who had somehow freed him at the top of the subway platform as he came out on the seventh day. He turned and tried to walk back down the escalator, but she had seen him, of course.

She waved so desperately that he realized what had happened: somehow, he must have transferred his curse to her. He was afraid to even talk to her. But the people behind him on the escalator wouldn't let him go the wrong way. Everyone had their own life to meet. They pushed him forward mercilessly, and then there she was. She was pretty, he realized suddenly, or would be if she did not look so depressed. He wondered if he was prettier now. Despite himself, he smiled sympathetically, but she seemed confused by his smile. She stepped toward him, and in her confusion, in her desperation, she stumbled. Her ankle twisted, and she fell forward. She was about to topple down the escalator—he had to do something. At the last moment, in good K-drama fashion, he pulled her toward him and away from certain injury. He held her safe. It took them both a second to realize that they embraced each other. Embarrassed, he released her and brushed off his hands on his jacket. He tried to calm his heart, which refused to slow. She seemed still in shock. People muttered with annoyance and swerved around them. She didn't move. Her eyes shone with such—relief?—or was it gratitude?—or maybe something like enchantment?—that he nearly, nearly, didn't notice that the future had returned to him and he was once again miserable.

5. A VISION

In fact, the moment Hwaeen saved Mirae from her fall, they shared a vision. This is where K-drama shines: in the tension between certainty and wonder. Is the vision their future, or is it some other connection between them and their imaginations? In the vision, they stood together in a beautiful green field, he in a black suit and tie, his hair slicked back, happy and handsome, and she in a black dress, with sunglasses and heels, also happy, though her happiness was hidden behind her lenses. They bowed together—but to whom? In the middle of the field, a hill marked someone's grave (had they come to pay respect?). Yet there was no morbidity or dread. They were happy together, happy to be together. They held hands and then leaned in, perhaps, for a kiss.

When they came out of the vision, both Hwaeen and Mirae felt confused. Both believed the vision to be theirs alone. But only Mirae felt free. The man who had saved her looked so sad that she actually wanted to take care of him. Yet a K-drama relies on its leads confusing their feelings until their hearts are completely entrapped. To put it simply: not wanting the ghost back, Mirae fled.

She got only a few steps, however, before she knew that the

ghost had once again followed her. She stopped. Hwaeen seemed to realize the same thing—on his back was no one, only air.

She returned to him.

He backed away.

"Help," she said.

The person she was in his vision...he saw her like that now, head high and beautiful, felt again that connection between them, the sense that he was going to kiss her. She was the same person asking him for his help.

"Don't go," she said. "Have coffee with me."

God help him, he nodded.

According to the rules of K-drama, as soon as he goes to her, he will do so again and again.

PART FOUR
WON

I. DUCKY DUCKY GOOSE

By the time All-Star Weekend rolled around, here was the situation: With only me leading, the team had gone 7–1; with both Powerball! and me, 0–5. Reporters said we couldn't play together. Since my contract would expire at the end of the year, the team could only get trade value for Powerball! The more people rumored about a trade, the worse the mood got in the locker room. Though Powerball! had supported me while he was injured, ever since we saw Robert Sung with his pants down, he had kept his distance. Coach was nervous about losing his job and for some reason (the reason was racism) he blamed me. The entire team was frustrated. Game by game, I felt my future contract shrink. Sung continued to praise Powerball! and write that the team should stay together as though he wasn't just afraid that a trade would take Brit away from him.

It was around that time—I remember it as before the All-Star Game, Carrie remembers it as after—that Carrie got fed up with Sung and called him out to his face. The three of us, without Ducky, who had canceled at the last minute, were out for dinner at a sundubu place in Flushing. We had almost finished when Sung's phone rang. His face reddened as if Asian flush had caught up to him all at once, and Carrie pursed her lips. I knew there was going to be trouble. Sung declined the call, but it was too late.

"When I was in high school," Carrie said, "a girl I knew killed herself. For weeks, she destroyed pencil cases, books, her favorite jewelry. She chipped the shellac off her desk little by little. Then she leapt off a building."

Sung downed his soju—which he had claimed to dislike, then drank two bottles of.

"Tell me you're not worried about Ducky," Carrie said.

I wondered when she had gotten to be such friends with Ducky or whether Ducky was in that bad shape.

"We're all adults." Sung stretched and drew in his shoulders like a bird folding in its wings before the storm.

Carrie scoffed. "Do you have some kind of white fetish, Robert?" she asked straight up.

I almost whistled.

Sung's nostrils flared.

"All right now," I said, raising an arm between them. "We cool?"

He reached across the table and I slapped his hand away. But he was only going for the water radish. He narrowed his eyes at me.

I wasn't afraid for Carrie. If he made any move toward her, she would rip him apart. A part of me wanted to protect *him.*

I said, "Ducky just came in."

He backed off.

I had wanted to see if she still meant something to him.

When he realized I had lied, he said, "Brit makes me feel like I got another chance at life."

"That's about you," Carrie said. "Not her. That's about yourself."

Sung squinted at me, pleading. "Haven't you felt like that, Won?" he asked.

Of course I had. But I wasn't taking sides against my girlfriend.

A stranger at another table waved, and I waved back at him so I wouldn't be called rude on somebody's blog.

"*You* understand," Sung said to me, "don't you?"

I said he and I were not the same.

Sung jerked back as if I had shot him. He looked so hurt that I nearly took it back. Yet I hadn't said anything that terrible. Had I? Without another word, not even leaving his share of the check, Sung slipped on his coat and slunk out the door. Whatever had made him so upset, it was clear that he thought I should regret it.

2. POWERBALL!'S STORY

After that dinner, Carrie showed me an email from Powerball! It was strange that PB would email her. He never emailed me. I hadn't thought he even used email, which made me realize I was prejudiced against him in some significant way.

It was a lengthy message. In his writing, he was not the efficient baller he was on the court. Or maybe he was playing the clock, winding the seconds down until he could take the final shot, get out with something irrevocable, a win or a loss. Outside of trash talk, Powerball! was never much of a talker. If a game started to slip away, he might fire us up in a time-out, or if we weren't in our spots, he might shout us into them, but most of the time, he spoke more to the other team, getting on their nerves and trying to break them down until he could see their cracks. His email held zero trash talk. He didn't lay a single insult on Sung, which made it even sadder. No wonder Carrie had felt the need to slash and burn at the restaurant. Powerball! cared about only Brit's feelings, no one else's. He told Carrie all about us going over to Sung's place with the eggs and kimchi, how he and I had squatted beneath the window, and in his straightforward prose, he finally confirmed that the naked woman facing away from the window had been his wife.

It was her back, he wrote. Maybe a woman can recognize any woman's back. A man can only recognize the back of the woman he loves. It was Brit. But you know, I think RS would of known her by her ass, too, the way he was standing. Dude wished to protect my wife, not his, not himself.

It was cringey, lovesick reasoning, but I could understand. It probably seemed like Sung was trying to replace Powerball! in his own life. Like Sung had planned out an extremely long revenge and, after years of praising PB to put off suspicion, was finally acting.

Instead of confronting Brit, Powerball! turned detective, checking her phone and her various designer bags. The nanny had caught him in one bag and grown so flustered that he knew immediately that she was on his wife's side. He had no evidence, yet there was no doubt in his mind. I fucking know, he wrote in the email. Feel like the animal in my chest keeps gnawing and gnawing, like I'm all bloody inside. I know what I know. She's been acting like a cheater for a month, since around when Won started starting, afraid to be herself.

At first, I thought Powerball! wanted to know if Carrie knew something he didn't—she was probably one of very few friends of both Brit and Ducky. But his email never asked a single question. There was nothing specific to Carrie at all. He was talking to himself. It was an email he could have sent anyone. Carrie asked how I thought she should respond, but it seemed more like she just wanted me to know there was cause for alarm. I remembered something she had said to me about the K-drama she was working on, that if people start acting out of character, they're either in love or about to die.

For the first time, I really worried about Powerball! It wasn't something I had ever thought I would do. On the court, he was so in control it didn't seem right for any of us to worry about him;

it wasn't our place. Instead, we worried about what he thought of us. Maybe no one except Brit and their kids had worried about him in a long time.

That possibility seemed so lonely to me that I admired PB even more. Alone, he kept going against the endless expectations and criticism, like the claim that he was just "not a winner," even after his long and historic career. He put the team on his shoulders; he shouldered the team's reputation. He kept working on his game, refining moves he had made a thousand times. Meanwhile, I couldn't take a single shot without my contract hanging over my head. Coach made it seem like I was one bad shot away from returning to the end of the bench.

I felt closer to PB, worrying about him. Maybe Carrie was right, and my worry meant I cared. I could imagine a tiny bit more of his world than I could before.

3. ANOTHER HIGH SCHOOL STORY

Robert Sung told me this story after the season was over. Maybe if he had told me earlier, it might have helped me understand him. It started with him falling in love with Brit at first sight, when she was still a freshman, before she became the most popular girl in school. That year, she had booked bigger and bigger commercials and modeling gigs until finally she had scored a role in a sitcom as a daughter too sexually developed for her age. By her sophomore year, her class had made her president, and she set out to make Powerball! (then Paul Burton) her boyfriend. According to Sung, Powerball! hadn't noticed her yet.

In other words, Sung thought that Brit had made up her mind from the beginning, that she had chosen Powerball! not for love but for their collective potential.

This made me wonder whether Sung really loved Brit at all, if he could think of her as that calculating. Maybe he would do anything to dismiss her marriage to Powerball! Whatever she felt back then, as Sung followed her around, whether his constant appeals ever got through to her, I had no idea. I thought they were using each other to work out their own insecurities, but maybe this was ungenerous. Sung said *he,* not Powerball!, was always there for her when she felt down. He was the only one who ever saw her cry, other than her parents. Some days, she would text him to meet her in the bell tower or an empty dorm room, and as soon as he got there, she would sob on his shoulder.

Still, Brit planned to romance Powerball! at the big end-of-the-year formal. Powerball! hated formals, since he couldn't afford a good suit and no one thought of a suit when they calculated what to give him to get a part of him in return. Brit hated the formals too, but she went. She had plenty of dresses—they appeared outside her room for weeks before each dance. She would research which shops the dresses came from and return them for cash. Before this dance, however, she used some of the money for a suit in Powerball!'s size—she had asked him what it was while pretending to joke about his height—and sent the suit to him anonymously with a note to meet the sender at the event.

The formals were a point of pride for rich parents, so each dance had the feel of a Disney ball. The richest parents fought to be the ones to donate the decorations, or the music, or the food, though none wanted to drive all the way in (or fly, in some cases) to chaperone. The school brought in crystal chandeliers—rented from where? or stored for these occasions?—and an ice sculptor to carve a bespoke punch fountain. A team of workers built the dance floors, and also unbuilt them, overnight.

These parties overwhelmed Sung, but he knew, by his puppiness, that Brit had something planned. So he got an embarrassing suit, too late to ask anyone, and went solo. He shuddered to think that without basketball he would be just another loser. He was afraid to be seen alone, but he was in love, and even unrequited love is a kind of company. Above all else, he didn't believe that Brit could harden her heart to him forever—he had seen how soft that heart was when she adopted a stray cat, or when she volunteered secretly at a nursing home, or when her eyes grew big at a gift of tulips, her simple favorite, before she drew determination again from that endless reserve of hers and rejected whatever boy had offered them.

When Sung got to the dance, it was nearly empty. It started at six, and he was there at seven, far too early. Only the unpopular kids were there, enjoying themselves before their oppressors would arrive. They knew how early to come to have their own fun and how early to leave before they became someone else's fun. As they danced and laughed together, Sung realized he didn't know a fraction of what they knew about how the school really operated. When you have to know something is when you know it thoroughly.

Sung looped the edges of the dance floor. No one waved or acknowledged him. In the center, a group of boys convened and danced completely in sync. After a while, Sung realized that he made the other kids nervous. He was circling them like a predator. They were confused why he was there, how the rules of engagement had changed.

Ashamed, he relocated to the hallway.

When the first group of popular kids arrived, it seemed like a relief. But as soon as one rich white boy sneered at him, Sung knew he couldn't be seen by them either. He didn't show his face again until Brit got there in one of the last groups. Powerball! still hadn't come: he had understood the rules better than Sung had.

As soon as Brit saw Sung, she pulled him into a corner, secreting him away to be alone together. His heart raced. He had waited for this moment. Finally, she saw him as he saw her and only the two of them mattered. "What are you doing here, Robbie?" she asked, using her latest pet name for him.

"I came for you," he said. "This thing is horrible. You must hate it here."

She seemed surprised, even though he always came for her. He could tell that he was right. An extra bit of stress tightened her face—he knew even the tautness of her skin. For a moment, she seemed about to admit it, to say, yes, she really did hate it, she really did feel alone and mistreated and wanted him by her side...

Then she shook her head as if she'd just forgotten herself.

"Why won't you feel your feels?" he said. "Why make things so complicated?"

She sighed. And somehow, in that sigh, he knew that she wouldn't hate it if he kissed her. She, too, remembered all the times they had held each other and given each other the comfort they didn't get elsewhere. He reached for her—and her arm responded, stroking the side of his head, the back of his neck, his shoulders. She moved closer to him. She breathed hot in the center of his chest—I figured that was the spot he always rubbed—and though nothing had happened yet, they were already panting.

In the end, however, they didn't kiss. She left him there and ignored him the rest of the night. He was crouched in that corner even now, still wondering what made her want Powerball! and not him.

Or maybe I'm projecting here.

By the following year, Brit and Powerball! were fawning all over each other. In Sung's heartsick heart, he believed that he had failed to protect her. He guarded that almost-kiss with the rest of his life. Even as Sung told me this story, I could tell that he considered it his duty to keep the memory alive—when Brit finally came to him, he seemed to think of the affair not as a disruption but as a continuation of that moment, which for him had never ended.

If the story stopped there, it would have been fine. It was his life. Yet Sung kept trying to connect all this to my stardom. What really creeped me out was the implication that the Wonder was what had finally allowed Brit to see him as a possible partner, as if she just needed to see another Asian American succeed. That he could think her love for him was conditional on my career was almost as sad as the fact that he could still want that love.

And yet—at the same time—I recognized the fear in that desire. For the two and a half seasons I sat on the end of the bench, I had worried that without basketball there would be nothing to distinguish me from any other Asian guy. That without basketball, I would be unlovable. I understood how Sung had felt at the dance before Brit arrived, like he didn't belong with either the outcasts or the popular kids. It was the same feeling that wouldn't let me believe I was an All-Star—even if, for a month, I had played as well as anyone in the league. When the votes came in and the talking heads acted like the Asian ballots shouldn't count, it was hard to shake the feeling that I thought I was at one dance when I was really at another.

4. BEFORE THE (WEEK) END

Powerball! and me were on the same flight for All-Star Weekend. As soon as we landed, we hit LA hard. We got in on Friday afternoon and Carrie didn't arrive until Saturday. She had given me this one night. I wanted to do up K-town K-style; drink wild, sing wild, maybe more, show off my hometown (no matter what, you're only voted into your first All-Star Game once). Powerball! wanted to party away from the other All-Stars, since he wanted to be treated as a superstar and not as a person, now that word was out about Brit and Sung—which humiliated PB a little too much, I thought, as if it hurt worse to be cuckolded by an Asian dude. He hated being as human as everyone else. Even with K-town giving us the worship we wanted, he kept shooting me a look that said did I really want to be mobbed by Koreans instead of drinking champagne in a private room in some nightclub like other A-listers, for wasn't I now an A-lister? I wanted to be reminded that people outside the circle jerk of our basketball lives liked us for our basketball lives.

K-town was one giant party, and we went bar to club to bar, followed the entire way. After six drinks for me and eighteen for Powerball!, we ended up at the dirtiest and most famous noraebang in LA. Any good night in K-town ends with karaoke. It was four in the morning, and we kept the place open. We took the biggest room and still it seemed small and packed and hazy and hot. There was smoke from cigars and blunts, and soju and expensive whiskey, and flashing lights coloring the smoke, and nudity from people we just met, and a sweet Korean woman who wanted to show me how much she liked my basketball, and women all over Powerball! too. The only thing holding me back from an all-out lovefest—the woman kept whispering in my ear, and I couldn't hear a thing, and it was the most pleasant sensation, her hand on my lap—was Powerball!'s numbface, like he just tolerated everything, like nothing mattered without Brit. My sad feeling for him was ruining my happy feeling for myself. I didn't mind sympathizing. I just didn't want to sympathize with him as I got my dick stroked.

"Dude," I said. "Look around you. This is the All-Star life, isn't it? This is the dream."

Powerball! leaned into my ear and said, "You're going to fuck her, aren't you?"

I was about to say, why shouldn't I and where did he get off anyway?—I had watched him pick up random women many times in the past—until I realized he wasn't guilting but encouraging.

"Stick your hand up her shirt," he said to me.

"Now rub her titty," he said.

One song ended and someone started singing "Sukiyaki."

I didn't know what to do. I didn't want to follow his directions, but I did.

I rubbed the woman's titty as she moaned into my left ear and he talked into the right—and though that should have taken the air out of my hard-on, I got harder. Something about the whole situation made me hot, like in K-town, even Powerball! wanted in on my action. I felt sexy, unrejectable. I was sandwiched between them: on my left, the woman had me in her hand in the smoke and the lights, and on my right, my teenage hero whispered to me. I wondered if he could see us. Maybe he couldn't really tell what was going on, the woman next to him rubbing on him and pulling him toward her. We each had our own thing, I mean. There was no reason he should have been paying attention to my thing.

"Pinch a little," he muttered as some stranger croaked about love. "Get your mouth down there and nibble it. Bite her on the nipple."

I did whatever he told me to do, as if I were not in control; he was. The woman squealed with pleasure, rabbitlike, which turned me on even more. I shivered. I was almost annoyed with us both for liking it so much, what Powerball! told me to do to her. I waited for him to tell me what was next. I didn't know what was going on, why I was so worked up. A tiny part of me worried that Carrie was right and I was really in love with Powerball!, but the rest of me just wanted to fuck.

"Put your hand down her pants," he said to me.

"What's your deal?" I asked. "Stop it."

"Put your hand down her pants," he said again, and I did it.

"Touch her clit," he said—and I heard the scorn now. I'd only missed it, or misheard it, before. I started to worry that was what had turned me on, that scorn.

I pushed her pants down.

"Fuck her right here," he said disdainfully.

"You're out of your mind," I said.

The woman pulled on my belt and turned me away from him, noticing the argument now. She didn't want me distracted. Her pride was suddenly at stake.

"You're out of your fucking mind," I said again, waiting for him to tell me what to do.

For an instant, it occurred to me that what he wanted was to swap bodies with me, as if he had mixed me up with Sung again, Sung who was fucking his wife, humiliating him. Sweat prickled my skin. I was afraid he would call me Robert.

"You the man," he said flatly. "Big man. You got her hanging all over you."

"I don't like the way you're talking," I said.

"You don't even care about Carrie."

The woman turned my chin with her hand. She squeezed my dick, angered. She raked a nail down my cheek, not softly, and squeezed me again even harder. Then she went down, right in the smoke and lights, and put me in her mouth.

"You the man," Powerball! said again. "You think you made it to my level, Won-derboy, just cause you got some Asian chick to suck you off in K-town?"

I wanted to punch him. *That's not my name,* I said—but only in my thoughts this time. I thought, *Forget him, this is happening to me.* Even if he was mixing me up in his imagination, I wasn't. I wasn't Robert Sung, and I wasn't him. The woman was doing this thing with her tongue I had never felt before.

Powerball! turned toward his other side, and now he went to town with the woman on him. But in the way they went to town, pointedly loud, he seemed to mock me for doing the same thing he had done his entire career.

"We have an open relationship," I managed to get out. "Carrie knows what goes on when we're on the road. She's not Brit."

Powerball! didn't answer, engrossed. He had already ruined everything so completely, though, that I could hear him anyway, saying did I even know who I was and what I wanted?

I wanted, suddenly, to look down at Carrie's face and see her disappointment in me. I felt pitiful and unresponsive.

The woman's neck stiffened, her pride pricked.

"I'm leaving with this girl," Powerball! said. "I don't respect no one that only goes halfway." He got up and they left together irreproachably.

I didn't know what the woman in my lap was going to do next. She didn't seem to know either.

5. THE DUNK CONTEST

Carrie was supposed to arrive with plenty of time before the dunk contest, which had been my favorite part of All-Star Weekend as a kid. But when I woke, I had two texts from her: the first said her plane needed maintenance and the second said she had been delayed and wouldn't get in until after the dunk contest started.

It was maybe three in the afternoon. I had time to get lunch and then head over to the Staples Center alone. It just didn't seem worth it. Each year, the dunk contest got more and more repetitive, the contestants risked less and less, and I grew further and further from my childhood. Seeing it by myself already sounded pathetic. I wondered whether I should visit my dad and sisters instead, who all lived south of LA now in Fullerton, with other Koreans who had made enough to get out. In K-town, my dad had run a law firm serving Korean businesses, mostly defending them against the city or big corporations. He had lost a lot but won enough. It was something to be embarrassed by as a teenager and proud of as an adult. I almost texted him before I realized that I should text one of my sisters instead. I texted my biggest noona, but she said Dad wasn't home and wouldn't be back until late. He's hiking with some other old people, she wrote. You know how they are. He's 100% ahjusshi now.

Should I visit you then? I texted.

We're all busy, she wrote back. She meant all the sisters—they often spoke like that, like they were a unit and I was the odd one out.

Do you, she texted.

Don't you have to do stuff before the game? she texted.

I was just trying to avoid Powerball! and whatever happened the night before. I still didn't know what that was. In the end, he had taken a woman back to the hotel and I hadn't. All night, I had dreamt that Carrie was in the noraebang, that she was the one getting me off. When I woke, alone, it was with a fist in my chest, pounding, like I was grieving. What was it that I had lost in that moment, other than my erection? Why did Powerball! get so pissed at me? It was a mystery I really did not want to solve. I wanted it to go away.

Carrie got to the hotel in time for a late dinner. Over dessert, she asked after Sung and Ducky—Ducky had argued her way onto the trip, though they hadn't planned for her to go. I hadn't seen either of them. Carrie said she had heard from Ducky that Ducky was monitoring her husband's phone for notifications, even holding off her bathroom trips as long as she could so as not to miss anything. "She's holding her pee in! That seems bad."

I thought cruelly that Ducky and Sung's main problem was that they hadn't broken up a long time ago. The most nerve-wracking moments in basketball are when the ball is in the air: before one team or the other gains possession, before a shot makes or misses. Sung was too weak to tell Ducky straight that he didn't love her. Brit had kept him hanging for a decade. I was starting to realize, without being able to put it into words or even a complete thought yet, that he had kept wanting Brit because she never told him she *didn't* want him.

"You look like you had sex last night," Carrie said.

I blushed. My whole body got hot, which made me blush even more, remembering how my body had gotten hot the night before.

"I'll take that as a yes," she said.

"I didn't."

She said there was no reason to lie and that lying only made it seem like cheating when it wasn't. I could have argued more, but there was no reason to believe me, either, and like she said, I hadn't done anything wrong. I didn't want to describe what *had* happened.

I wondered why, then, I felt so sorry.

Carrie said she heard that Powerball! had helped out with the dunk contest even though he wasn't billed as a contestant. As she left LAX, she overheard a group talk about how Powerball! had walked onto the court from the crowd and assisted one dunk after another, until it wasn't clear whether he was part of the plan or not.

That really puzzled me. Powerball! wasn't the type to throw light on a rival's dunk. Carrie and I went up to the room and found the footage on YouTube. To the average viewer—at least, judging from the comments—it looked like Powerball! had stepped on court with one purpose and then, halfway there, changed his mind. He had tried to make his appearance on court *seem* purposeful by helping out.

I stopped the video at the exact moment Robert Sung appeared on-screen, just one head among the many, except on wider shoulders. When I pointed him out to Carrie, we agreed that the look on his face was terror. Powerball! must have gone for him on national TV and stopped only when he realized he was on national TV.

"Be careful out there," Carrie said. "Paul Burton looks like a different person."

I nodded, hearing that different person in my ear.

6. STAR TURN

Before the game, Sung sent me a text that he was keeping his distance from Powerball! but he had something to tell me. I was in the locker room, getting changed into my All-Star uniform. I had dreamt of putting on that uniform ever since I was a kid. I wondered how often someone achieved a dream like that.

What happened in the dunk contest? I texted back. On YouTube, it looked like PB was going to kill you.

Sung sent back an emoji of a face blue and frozen. You saw that?

I saw.

I watched the three dots move that meant he was typing something. Nothing came.

RS? I texted.

Finally, the dots moved again. Watch your back. Off the record.

It was strange how he had picked up the habit of saying that, *on* or *off the record,* as if he was not a reporter but one of the sources that record was supposed to protect.

What do you mean? I texted.

It's not just me PB is after. Off the record.

As soon as we got on the court, I knew something was wrong.

My teammates for the day had turned against me. They wouldn't even call me by my nickname. I didn't know why. I was a little kid again, trying out the nearby Montessori school, where the other kids wouldn't play with me because they had all agreed I wasn't like them.

I was determined not to let it get to me. No one could take away the fact that I was an All-Star or disregard the millions of people who voted for me.

What really hurt was Powerball! In the pregame huddle, as everyone circled, he stood beside me but wouldn't touch me. He lifted his arm from my back and shook my arm off his back—and the guy on my other side did the same—and I was alone even as I was surrounded. We grunted and walked out, but I knew then that I had only a couple of minutes before Coach Brown took me out and replaced me with someone else. I was the point guard, so I expected to get the ball in my hands at least once. Yet we lost the tip, and the inbounds pass went straight to Powerball!, as if I wasn't there, and he threw an oop to D-White, and then the West scored and the inbounds pass went to someone else... and I never got a hand on the rock before I ended up on the bench. Sitting there felt even worse than it used to feel when no one knew me. Even the Asian American press would have to report that I had played only three minutes with zero points, zero rebounds, zero assists, and so on.

At the next time-out, I tried to get Powerball!'s attention. "I didn't fuck her," I whispered, using the word he had used. "I'm not the one sleeping with your wife." By then, I understood that he was taking out on me his anger at Sung. He wanted to humiliate Sung, so he humiliated me. It was enough to condemn me that I was also Powerball!'s teammate, also a point guard—and most of all, I thought, also Korean. Powerball! pretended he didn't hear me, and a camera caught us before I could say anything else. I looked up into the crowd: Carrie wore a worried frown, Sung mouthed a question I couldn't understand. But I was the one who had to sit there as if I was invisible, feeling as if everyone's eyes were on me except for the eyes of the other All-Stars.

By halftime, Powerball! had our side up by twenty. For an All-Star Game, he played meanly. Usually, players goofed around and tried not to get injured. He dominated recklessly. Everyone seemed anxious, reluctant to give him the ball but more afraid not to. In the second half, not wanting to watch anymore, I spotted Ducky six rows above Sung's assigned press seat, her stare fixed on the back of his head. For several plays, her eyes didn't move at all, except to blink. Baskets came and went. I sat on the bench, staring at her, and she sat in the stands, staring at her husband. After a while, her dedication to their marriage moved me as it never had before. Even if they started to hate each other, I saw, she would still want to be with him. Coach called a time-out and I didn't even bother to join the huddle. Whistles blew. I admired Ducky's devotion so much that shame and pity welled. I was about to cry over a white woman during the All-Star Game. I shook my head. My teammates seemed to glance over at me now each time Powerball! went wild, at first with a kind of blame, then pleading, like *Didn't I know what to do about him? Wasn't I used to this?*

In the end, Coach Brown sat Powerball! on the opposite end of the bench from me, closest to the assistant coaches. Powerball! shook with anger—the reverberation traveled down the row of seats to my thighs. When a camera found him, though, he managed a fake smile.

As soon as the camera moved away, I slid next to him.

"You're an asshole," he said. "You should of fucked her." He switched to the seat I had left, all the way back down the bench. What did he want from me?

I played two more minutes, all garbage time, and finished with one missed shot and a broken ego, but my mind wasn't on the game. It was on the data: Powerball!'s scorn in the noraebang, his participation in the dunk contest, Sung's text, my teammates uniting to embarrass me. Powerball! got the game's MVP. As he lifted the trophy over his head, the other All-Stars talked shit, disgusted at him for playing selfishly and almost causing two injuries. Carrie was right: Powerball! had changed. The Powerball! I knew would never sacrifice a teammate for a game that meant nothing to our record. This Powerball! didn't give a shit about anyone. He glared into the stands. I thought Brit must have shown up and he had played that way for her. But when I followed his stare, there was Ducky. He had noticed the same thing I had, that she had eyes only for Sung. She didn't even realize Powerball! was looking at her. I wondered whether he was jealous of her love or whether he identified with it, with her. The whole weekend was so confusing and seemed so significant that I barely noticed what the newspapers said about me the next day. I just wanted my arms around the person I loved.

7. GLORY

I got out of the Staples Center after only a couple of dejected interviews with foreign reporters who spoke through translators and skipped over how badly I'd played in the All-Star Game to ask how the Knicks would do in the second half of the season. In the tunnel, Carrie waited for me. She hit her chest with her fist in the Korean way, as if it hurt her physically to think of me in the locker room surrounded by eleven players who had just humiliated me.

"That was awful," she said. "What a fucker. How could Paul turn everyone against you like that? You've been nothing but loyal to him."

I felt numb in the center of my back, and the feeling slowly spread across my skin. *I am going to be angry,* I thought, but anger didn't come. What came was pity and dread. Even with a career like his, Powerball! still felt threatened by the idea of an Asian dude taking his place. That was the reason he saw Robert Sung when he looked at me: yellow peril. On some level—the level of race—Powerball! still didn't trust me. It was shitty and lonely.

Carrie led me out of there. She drove us back to the hotel in her rental car, and we ate in the hotel restaurant. I had no energy for anything else. All the excitement of being an All-Star was gone. Dinner tasted like rubber.

As I complained, I reached for Carrie's hand again and again. It was dry from the cold winter air and the back-and-forth flights and, probably, stress. She seemed amused by this tenderness, though not in a bad way. She listened and squeezed my hand. We both realized that I needed, for some reason, to feel our skin meet, to close the gap between us. We ate one-handed, even fed each other a few bites of fettucine.

"Want me to beat him up for you?" Carrie asked. She dropped her fork and threw a left jab in a beautifully straight line. Her eyebrows furrowed and a crease appeared on her nose bridge. "I know it's a cliché, but I'm a second-degree black belt."

"I believe you," I said. "I'm thankful you're on my side."

"I'd need both hands though. You'd have to let go." She leaned toward me now and met my stare. "I feel like this is making you horny," she said.

"You feel like it makes me horny to imagine you beating him up?"

She smiled, showing her dimples.

All desire, I thought, *is a triangle.*

I couldn't help but remember the noraebang.

I said that, at the end of the All-Star Game, when Powerball! got his trophy, he was looking up into the stands at Ducky. "Weird, right? It was like he was staring into a mirror. Like by feeling bad for her, he could feel bad for himself."

Triangles.

Before home games—I had seen this a number of times—Powerball! would psych himself up by growling at a mirror taped inside his locker. Who was he trying to intimidate, I wondered every time—himself? I often looked for the third person, the one that wasn't him.

Carrie shook her head no. She said I must have made a mistake, Ducky had texted her at halftime. She showed me the texts: Can't watch anymore. Going back to hotel. U must feel bad for won.

"You must have seen a different white woman," Carrie teased.

I wished I had, but I knew what I had seen. I too had a text. Sorry, it said. I told Powerball I couldn't keep writing that the Knicks should keep him if it's him fucking up, not u. Looks like he was out to prove me wrong.

I had texted Sung back: So you told him it was him versus me? You are the worst and I'm sorry to know you.

"Carrie," I said. "Tell me why you love me."

"That's a K-drama trope. The question says more about the person asking than the person answering." She lifted my palm, the one holding hers, to my cheek so that I cupped my own face with her hand on top of mine.

"I see you," she said.

"What?"

"Just *I see you.*"

She tucked her chin down and gazed at me from the tops of her eyes, without saying a word. I felt a tremble in my chest, and then my whole body quivered, quaked. I dropped my hand to my lap and tried to steady it.

"Are you okay?" she asked.

I said, "Can we forget this 'open relationship' stuff? Let's get married or something."

"Or something," she said. With her hand now free, she touched my forehead as if to check my temperature. She pressed her thumb between my eyebrows. "You have a line there, like a dent, when you get upset."

I took a deep breath. "I'm not upset. I'm serious."

She nodded. "I know. Anyway, don't take it back. It was very sweet."

I wasn't going to take it back. I would never. I was still vibrating with being seen, being held by her gaze, beheld. I wanted a life worth being seen for.

"Be honest now," Carrie said. "Did you sleep with someone the other night?"

The answer she wanted was yes, and it was simpler than trying to explain the feeling shaking my heart.

8. RUN-INS WITH WHITENESS

Back in New York after All-Star Weekend, I ran into a fan on Ninth Avenue, a white dude wearing my jersey over his coat, in the cold. The Knicks were making millions off my name, my number, putting it on any piece of clothing they could. None of that money came to me. I had splurged a fifth of my salary on the Escalade that I rarely drove, except to the practice facility. In the city, it was faster and easier to catch a ride—one of the things I could do that Black players rarely did. I needed the contract to come through and confirm that I was worth the kind of money that would allow me to live that Escalade life. I was guaranteed nothing until I signed a long-term deal to stay in New York, which everyone said would happen and no one would promise. I wanted to know what my fan thought about how his money went to the NBA, the team, the distributor, the merchant, etc., etc., and not me. I wanted, basically, to confront him with my reality. To make him see me and not my number.

"Nice duds," I said.

He jumped back, and I saw that I had had an effect. He was a little guy with a certain hawkishness about him, like at any moment he might tell you about a war he'd been in.

"What the hell?" he said as if he hadn't seen me there.

I waited.

"You're a Wonderboy fan, huh?" he said.

I thought he was joking at first, doing a white-guy bit, looking down on me even though he was literally looking up. I smiled to put him at ease, doing my Asian-guy bit.

"I guess all of you are Wonderboy fans," he said sincerely.

I had kind of thought that at that time any tall Asian dude was getting asked if he was me. White people say we all look alike because they really can't tell the difference—what they mean is *they* don't know how to look. I thought maybe this guy was so sensitive to his own racism that he couldn't even assume I was the guy on his jersey.

"I'm Won," I said, putting out my hand, trying to give him an excuse to correct himself.

"You even got the same name. Must be common?"

He stepped back.

He wasn't putting two and two together though, he just wanted to be a little farther away from me.

Suddenly he shook like something had reached up from under the ground and was pulling him down into hell. He shook like he had to get out of its grip. He pulled off his jersey and coat—underneath he wore a black T-shirt that read *Be Calm and Love Each Other*—and he yelled "cockroach" at me and shook and shook.

Cockroach, I thought, *where have I heard that before?*

Then I saw a cockroach scuttle away. The white dude jabbed a finger at it, and I realized that he meant a real cockroach and also that the cockroach had accomplished what I had not: confronted him with its reality.

As I left the guy standing there and got into my ride, I was reminded of my freshman roommate, Alvin, a white scholarship kid, a real farm-boy genius. He was the smartest kid I ever knew. He had to be, to get in against the legacy kids. He was the smartest not about books or life or any particular subject—he was the smartest about the stuff most of us didn't want to think about. He would tell me, for instance, about how many rooms were in the dorm and how many dudes there were and how many were probably masturbating at that moment and how many mice were in the walls looking for food and how many more bugs were scurrying around looking for warmth and how our little dorm room was basically a bubble we lived in to pretend like there was an inside and an outside, an us versus everything else, when that everything else made up much more of the world than we did, and he would tell me that the school was like that too, a bubble, and all the people we knew, and even all the people they knew, etc., were still just a small bubble. One day, he told me that even if every human being in the world came together, if the bugs turned on us, they could eat us all in a few seconds, before we would even know to fight back. Instead, they just lived their lives, which were the real lives, the same lives other animals and plants were living, just effing life.

We thought we were so special, was his point.

I was reminded of Alvin, though, not because of his mind, but because one day, we had a roach infestation. It seemed like a sudden thing, like all the cockroaches had shown up at once, yet of course I knew, as Alvin knew, that they had been there all along and that the infestation was really a spike in our awareness of them. We saw three cockroaches in an hour, and then the whole damn place was sprayed and fumigated and so on, to make the rest of the world disappear for us again, to make our bubble stronger and more opaque, harder to see through. But those three cockroaches—Alvin killed them one by one without any word or reaction. He killed them before I even saw them. His foot just moved out and then moved back, and a dead cockroach would be lying there. Once he finished reading or googling or whatever, he would clean the roach up. After the fumigation, he was at his most scoffing toward the rest of us, so I asked about his killer instinct. He said he was just speaking their language, acknowledging how they lived, kill or be killed, and more than that, he was speaking our language, acknowledging that they only died if they showed themselves. Then he said what I would never forget, and never forgive him for, because I had thought of him as a friend, I guess, up until that point. He said, "You get it, don't you? Don't you live with that all the time?"

As a gook, I thought when I figured out what he meant. *Don't I live with the threat of getting stomped on as a gook?*

And sure, I did. They hated us, white folks, only when they had to notice us, when they had to notice that the world was bigger than just them, when they saw for a second through their bubbles the way the world was built up for them on the bodies of black people, brown people, red people, yellow people, all the people like bugs who lived our real lives to create the beautiful unreality of theirs.

I wished I could contact Alvin now. He had killed himself. He couldn't take it, living in that real world, knowing what it was like. He did it the year after we graduated—my big noona came across his obituary and remembered the odd boy who had come home with me once over a break and pointed out to my family our various levels of ignorance. I wished I could tell Alvin about the cockroach man. He would have laughed and laughed.

My driver stared at me in his rearview mirror. When I met his eyes, he pinched his nose. I wanted to ignore him, but I felt, in honor of Alvin's memory, that I couldn't.

"Yes," I said. "It's me."

"You really stunk in the All-Star Game, man," he said. "For a while, I thought you weren't never going to lose, and now look at you, taking a Lyft home."

He said it like he thought I had a private limo.

"You know they're not going to sign you, right? You got to bring that Wonder back."

I didn't answer. I wasn't going to get pissed off and show up in a video on YouTube.

Would the Knicks really not sign me? I felt chilled. It was possible, if they thought Powerball! didn't want me there. In a single month, my life had gone from no one knowing me to everyone loving me to no one wanting me to be an All-Star. I had to bring the Wonder back, the driver had said. The Wonder. Even Carrie called those wins the Wonder. She said it was about possibilities, like if there could be an Asian American basketball star, there could be other things we were capable of that we never thought we were. Why did we think we weren't capable?

I remembered a story Powerball! had told me once about the first time he took Brit to his parents' house. It was before his rookie season, while Brit was pregnant but before they married. With his signing bonus, he had bought his parents a house in Jersey. He and Brit went to get his parents' approval the old-fashioned way. His parents hardly knew Brit. They'd rarely visited the boarding school, and only to see his games. The whole drive down, he warned her they might not approve, they might think that just when he had finally achieved everything they wanted from him, he was going to give it away to someone else. Even pregnancy, he worried, they might take as a threat. But Brit said he wasn't giving them enough credit—they had raised him, after all, and he had turned out all right.

His parents gave them an enthusiastic greeting, said they had seen the films Brit was in, she was so beautiful in them, they hoped she would take care of their son and grandchild. At first, it seemed like Brit was right. Yet the more his parents complimented her, the worse those compliments felt. Again and again, his mom pointed out Brit's eyebrows and hair and lipstick color. When his dad said how good the lighting was in Brit's films, Powerball! realized that they were commenting on her whiteness. He made a big show of saying he didn't like Brit for her looks, listing the things he did like: her drive, her confidence, her smarts, her acting... They waited for more. To break the tension, Brit joked, "I am very beautiful though," and smiled weakly. The rest of the night was full of quiet disdain.

Why couldn't we see ourselves? Powerball! had told me this story as a possible Where the Relationship Went Wrong. He said Brit had been disappointed in him ever since that day. He tried to blame his parents, in other words, yet it was clear he didn't believe himself. He scratched his ear. I had never thought he was the kind of person who needed to lie to himself. I raised my hand to his shoulder, and he brushed it off. So, I thought, it wasn't just Asians who got confused around a white person as if we were the ones, somehow, who had worked ourselves into a false position. I had thought that confusion was our thing. I had thought that bubble was ours.

9. IN BALL, THE PAST IS NEVER THE PAST

On the way home, I got a text from Robert Sung, and after some self-conflict, I redirected my ride to Crown Heights. With hindsight, I can see now that Carrie was right about the strange identification between Sung and me—I must have given him another chance because it felt like giving myself another chance. Sung was high and rewatching the All-Star Game, marveling at Powerball! as usual. He sat on their Scandinavian couch, cross-legged, and I sat in the matching chair, feeling weird about wearing my shoes inside, like we weren't both Korean. I was still pissed about how he had set Powerball! against me, especially as it was clear from the way he mooned at the TV that he never thought I was on Powerball!'s level. I had been trying to figure out why he did it, and I had concluded that he was pissed at me too. He must have been angry that I had taken Powerball!'s side and not his, with regard to his little affair. Maybe—the thought crossed my mind—he had even said what he said to drive a wedge between Powerball! and me. He probably didn't know that this was the same strategy by which the model minority myth attempted to drive a wedge between Asian and African Americans.

"Where's Ducky?" I asked. "You kick her out already?"

He ignored this question. He pointed to the TV, where Powerball! spun around one defender and went up and under another. "See that move," Sung said. "That was his signature move in high school, and he never had to change it. Even if you know it's coming, you can't do anything to stop it."

I knew the move. I wished it didn't impress me as it still impressed Sung—but it was, in fact, amazing that a thing Powerball! figured out as a kid could serve the same purpose for so long.

"Why am I here?" I asked. "You said you needed to tell me something." I still expected an apology.

Finally, Sung looked at me. He had bags under his eyes and a couple of days' worth of stubble. He shivered as if I had opened a window, and his shoulders heaved. "I'm going to bury him," he said softly, his eyes wet with resolve. "I can't let Brit go back to him."

"What?"

"She won't go back to him if his reputation is ruined."

All around the living room, things were decorated to Ducky's taste, as if he didn't live there, though he was the only one home now; maybe Ducky was at a friend's apartment. "Don't you think you're being unfair to Brit," I asked, "thinking of her like that? I mean she's clearly not with you because of your success."

I couldn't help myself.

He gritted his teeth. "Shouldn't you be worried about PB, not Brit? He's your teammate."

But we weren't on the best of terms at the moment, thanks to someone.

"Anyway," he said. "I'm just letting you know, because you saw how he can be."

"Is that why you asked me here?" I said, realizing. "To what? Warn me that the All-Star Game was just the beginning? What the fuck?"

"Look," he said. "I'm sorry, Won."

I was shocked at how genuine he sounded.

"You should protect yourself."

"Are you giving me advice right now?" I asked. "Really?"

"Just listen for a second," Sung said, "to someone older than you. You're here, after all."

I had made the mistake of going there, he meant. The mistake of believing again in some Korean connection between us. *Jung* or something.

"I've been in your position," he said.

"You haven't been in my position."

He went quiet. His eyes were red, only partly from the weed. "No," he said. "You're right. I guess that's the point. You got a different chance than I had. I don't even know how I ended up in this life."

"I'm just a basketball player," I said. "I don't get it."

He clicked his little pen—I didn't even know he'd taken it out. When had he done that?

"Wait a second," I said. "This isn't an interview. This is all off the record, you bastard."

"You always play dumb," he said, "when it's convenient for you."

He grabbed a notebook from the side table and wrote something in it. "Look." He had written, *Carrie isn't good enough for you.* Nothing else.

"You're wrong," I said.

"It doesn't matter if I'm wrong or not," he said. "What matters is that as soon as you're told something"—he tapped his temple—"it gets into your head. That's why you got to protect yourself."

It was my fault for expecting more from him.

On the TV screen, Powerball! stepped back, crossed over, broke ankles. The defender fell on his ass. I remembered this moment and the excitement the poor guy's humiliation had infused into the arena. Fans wanted blood.

"He stole that move from Kobe," Sung said absently.

"Who stole it from someone else," I said. "Who stole it from someone else."

Sung continued to watch the All-Star Game as if my presence made no difference to him. I could have walked straight out the door without him noticing. Ducky would never get through to him; he was already lost to the present. I could have ripped his entire notebook to shreds and he would have kept right on watching. I could have yelled, "Cockroach!" and pointed to the floor, and one part of him would have reached out a foot to crush the imaginary bug while the rest of him never strayed from where he was.

10. HISTORY REDEFEATS ITSELF

When we got back to New York after the All-Star break, Powerball! stopped being an asshole to me, because he stopped caring about anything that wasn't Brit. It was like the weekend had never happened. After our first game back, an L, he texted me a video of Sung and Brit—he had paid a PI to follow her. In the video, I saw a new side of Sung. He doted on Brit down to the smallest detail: at one point, he seemed to raise his hand and then I noticed that he was blocking the sun from her eyes. I could see why she would like him, though I wasn't sure why he liked her, unless it was simply to return to the past. I asked Powerball! not to send me illegal surveillance. He said it wasn't illegal, just secret, but he complied. I didn't know how to talk to him about the All-Star Game.

Maybe he didn't even think about it. He moped constantly now. No one on the team was used to it—Powerball! had always kept his private life carefully cordoned off. Maybe he had texted friends on other teams, other superstars, but in our locker room, he had led by the example of absolute focus. As that focus disappeared, or rather shifted to the affair between his wife and Sung, what made him so great seemed to disappear too. It was hard to believe that he was the same person: how had we fallen under the spell of someone so sad and obsessed?

I blamed Sung. The rest of the team blamed me.

The really remarkable thing was that Powerball! continued to put up twenty-plus points a game. He did it on autopilot. The difference would have been difficult for casual fans to spot. He still got his numbers; he just never led us to victory anymore. We couldn't count on him to take over the end of a game. He seemed to have given in to his reputation as not a winner.

I waited for Sung to carry out his threat to "bury" Powerball!, whatever that meant. But maybe he'd changed his mind. Maybe he wanted to be a better person. Either way, nothing seemed to happen. I didn't bring it up to him. I had enough to worry about with my contract undecided and the team unsure if I was now their leader or what.

My agent urged me to play like before, but I couldn't get that same spark back. The anger and injustice I had felt in my fingertips, I now had to call up from memory. During the Wonder, it had felt like me against the world. I couldn't feel that way with Powerball! around. It was like crying underdog when you had a ten-point lead. I tried to think of Powerball! as an extremely good role player, but the defense didn't react to him like that. They hovered around the spaces he liked best, making it harder to use those spaces for anything except to get him the ball.

We were still in each other's way. Eventually, one of us was bound to get injured. In the middle of March, in a game against the Nets, I had the ball at the end of the half as the clock ticked down, and I wanted those last points to give us momentum going into halftime. My man had been muttering racist shit all game long, so I also wanted revenge. I waved off my teammates until it was me and him. Softly, so that only I heard, he said that he was going to fuck my mother—who was dead.

At that point, there was this idea in the league that I could only go right, so I knew I could cross him over, go left, and get to the rim. With ten seconds left, the fans started to count down. "At five," I said, "I'm going to embarrass you." I wanted him to bite hard at my first step. He was already overplaying my right.

At five, I faked right with my shoulder down, and he fell for it completely. He jumped over to take the charge. I was already going the opposite way. He had leaned back to make it easier to flop and got caught teetering on his heels, trying not to land on his ass.

I drove into the lane, but the defense collapsed. I went up for a floater and double-clutched. My eye was on the basket the entire time, so I wasn't looking where I landed. My foot came down on something hard, and my leg twisted at the same time as the pain exploded in my knee...and then I was on the floor, trying not to cry too much.

The stretcher came out—I saw this later, on TV—and I knew that my season was over. I hoped it wasn't my career. Someone next to me said, "Oh shit, oh shit" and "I'm sorry," or variations thereof, over and over. I had landed on Powerball!'s foot, as if that was always how things were going to turn out. As if that was his fate with any Asian American baller.

I didn't blame him though. He didn't do it on purpose. He was so out of it, as I said, thinking only of Brit. Coach had even warned him to get his head in the game or else someone could get hurt. That someone was me. I was pretty sure I didn't blame anyone. Carrie said that on TV, it looked like an accident, not a malicious attack, and no one wrote or said anything in the news that indicated it was anything else. The only doubt came from Robert Sung. He visited me in the hospital, visibly upset. His wide shoulders drooped and his eyes were puffy.

"I can't believe PB did that shit again," he said. "I told you to protect yourself."

I said weakly that it was an accident.

"It was an accident that PB stuck his foot under his only two Asian teammates and busted both of their knees?"

That was exactly what I had told myself, but it sounded worse when he said it.

Obviously, I saw the same coincidences he saw. It annoyed me that he could act like I didn't.

"Why don't you write about it then, Robert?" I said. "If you're sure. You said you were going to bury him."

"Aren't you scared?" He smoothed back the hair over his ears, which made his eyes look bigger.

I hadn't considered this. Was I scared? Maybe ever since his own knee got injured, Sung had been afraid. But then why follow Powerball!'s career for so long and continue to hit on Brit?

He was afraid of *something,* but an idea nagged at me that it wasn't Powerball! What more could Powerball! do to him? The idea was that Sung was afraid that Powerball! *hadn't* tried to hurt him, that Powerball! had never considered him that important at all.

"I'm going to get Carrie to elope with me," I said.

He looked at me like what was I talking about, out of the blue?

"Your note," I explained. "You said she isn't good enough for me. I'll show you that doesn't work on me. That's just you. You're the one who's afraid."

"He ruined your knee," Sung said. "What is wrong with you?"

It was me who should have been asking him that, I thought. Why did he keep coming to me and telling me to choose sides? I wasn't taking either side, any side. I was choosing myself.

PART FIVE
CARRIE

I. INTERNMENT

K was reading the books I left her, books about cancer and death and love. The book she liked best was about all three, written by an academic who, as soon as she is diagnosed, finds the academic world small and stifling. What strikes her most about her sickness is that it works against its own interests. Cancer wants to thrive and live forever, but it can live forever only if it doesn't thrive—its survival in the body means the body's death. Since it isn't contagious, it can't transfer to another body; only petri dishes, only science, can keep it alive on its own. Basically, the rules are the same as in basketball: the body and cancer can't be in the same place at the same time. But what the academic says isn't that the body needs to get free, it's that between the body's self-destruction and its need to survive, there is something like love.

K told me all this from her hospital bed before another chemo treatment. Her husband Fred and I sat side by side on the bench/cot beside her. Fred hated that I left these books—he had emailed and then texted me that I needed to stop. But need was a funny thing. It was clearly *his* need that he meant. He was of the opinion that K should avoid any bad feelings at all, both for her own mental health and for others'. K explained that his parents and grandparents had taken this approach after World War II, never complaining about the camps and trying to avoid talking about them altogether. "So Fred thinks his family's silence turned out okay?" I asked. "Of course not," K said. "He hates that they do that. But that's the response he learned."

I wanted everyone to let my sister feel whatever she felt. What I knew about the kind of love K described, between self-destruction and survival, was what I knew about K-drama. Romance lives on the edge of a blade on which one side is rejection and the other desire. What Westerners call "chemistry" is really a passion convincing enough that we can feel that edge.

"I want you to hold my funeral," K said now, "before I'm too dead to appreciate it."

Fred flinched. Lately K kept asking, "Is this even life?" which at first I took rhetorically, like *Living this way isn't worth it*—before I realized she meant it literally, like *Am I alive or not?* She had rapidly lost most of her flesh. Her skin hung over her bones like a sheet over a drying rack. We could see the life draining out of her, little by little, in a way that made it clear to me, at last, that there is something separate from the body, some aura or energy. A dieter who loses a hundred pounds is no less alive. Even without the weight loss, K had less life: not less life to live, but less of whatever life was inside her.

It turned out she had planned the entire funeral already, had called a church and gotten the priest on her side, had chosen the flower arrangements, the Bible verses, the people to give eulogies. I looked at Fred like how did he not know any of this? Each time I tried to talk to him for real, he refused to say or even hear the word *dying*.

But he did know—they had made some of the funeral plans together—he just didn't know she meant to host the funeral herself.

"We bought our caskets and plot when we got married," Fred said morosely. "Maybe that was bad luck."

"He's been planning my death from the beginning," K said.

Since Fred didn't laugh, I had to.

He gave me the finger, clueless that K was joking for his sake, not hers. There was nothing I could do for him.

"At least he fed me," K said. "Good thing I was fat before, or there'd be nothing left of me now."

"Try to relax before the chemo," Fred said.

But once the chemicals got in her, she was always in too much pain to talk.

"I don't want to do chemo anymore," K said. "You don't know what it's like. The chemo is the worst part."

"You've got to."

I kicked his foot. This was exactly what must piss her off. Unlike in K-drama, dying didn't make them understand each other—Fred wanted K to feel okay about leaving us so she could have a "good" death. K wanted Fred to toughen up so he could have a "good" life once she was gone.

"What?" Fred said. "What did I do so wrong?"

K started to cry. Again.

I climbed onto the bed and held her until she stopped. Her bones poked into me, her skin loose and wrinkled like an old woman's. From the bench, Fred radiated guilt. When I looked over, he had his head between his knees.

"I want to know what it's like to be dead," K said, "while I still can. There's a line in the book—what was it again?—something like, 'By the time you die, it's too late to figure out how you feel about dying'..." In my ear, she whispered, "Maybe I'll love him again if I see him cry over my death."

A nurse came in with the chemo machine, which looked like how people in the eighties thought the future would look, a box on a pole with a bunch of switches and cords and a small computer screen.

"Promise me," K said as the nurse hooked up the IVs. "I want to see everyone together. What's the point of getting together when I'm dead? The oppas haven't visited me at all."

I promised. We would have promised her anything that would give her the least bit of comfort.

It surprised me that our three older brothers hadn't visited. Even if they had lives and families of their own, and lived hours away, I had assumed they visited K when I wasn't there. Typical that the women do the emotional lifting while the men buy the coffin and carry it only until they can put it in the ground. Growing up, our brothers had been a unit of their own, rarely letting K and me play with them. If anyone messed with us, though, they were vicious and unforgiving. When the family moved from LA to New York after the Sa-I-Gu riots destroyed Dad's shop, our brothers were suddenly California cool. They liked to pretend they were Korean Tupac or something. They had thought of themselves as protectors. What were they protecting now?

While K fought death, I told her stories from our past. The memory that came to me first was when she broke my arm, the day after we all went to the circus. We were playing dolls on the top bunk of the bed we shared, and with no warning, she shouted, "Acrobat!" and pushed me off. She looked so shocked when I didn't perform a trick, as if it was my fault. In those days, she hurt me many times this way, acting as if I was already a part of the game in her head. I wished I knew what was in her head now.

2. FREEDOM IS CROWDFUNDED

For much of March, I stood witness to the body's betrayals. K needed to gain weight but could barely manage a bite of any meal. Won spent hours in physical therapy, afraid of becoming Robert Sung, his injury hanging over his return and his contract. Watching their struggles, I decided there were enough limits on the physical body without being limited by the body other people imagined. I couldn't wait any longer to make the basketball K-drama my company had told me not to make.

In order to get free, I did what everyone did at that time to pay for their dreams or their tragedies: I started a crowdfunding campaign. I hired a PR consultant with my own money. We set prizes, we found media outlets eager to announce anything they could call "diverse." The publicist was a Korean American genderqueer influencer named Lex, who had wanted a show like this their entire life. Like my mom and Robert Sung, they were adopted. They were the first adoptee I knew who was in reunion with their birth family. They had gotten into K-drama to learn the language and culture, and instead, they said, they had learned how to forgive their birth mom. ("Wish I had something to teach me how to forgive my white mom," they joked, which was how I knew we would get along.) The only thing we disagreed about was whether or not to involve Won. Won would attract free publicity, yet I didn't want to use or compromise his stardom.

By the end of the first week, we had only five hundred thousand dollars, which was a quarter of our minimum goal and a tenth of what we needed. Lex insisted we should make use of all our resources—meaning my relationship. But was a boyfriend a *resource*? I told Lex about a film I liked in which the main character, a gangster, uses someone who has a crush on her to do bad things she doesn't want to come back to her. At the end of the film, she apologizes to him. "I'm sorry I acted like I didn't know you liked me," she tells him, "but if I knew, I would have had to stop using you, and I couldn't do that." She thinks she is confessing the worst thing she's done to him. But he says, "I knew you were pretending. All I could do to show you how much I liked you was to let myself be used, so I was thankful that you kept asking me to do things."

"See?" Lex said.

I said that conversation doesn't bring them together; it's what they say to each other just before he dies for her.

Love isn't a resource unless you're willing to use your lover up.

"Wow," Lex said. "Way to put the *drama* in K-drama."

Then one morning, Lex called at 6:00 a.m. and said we had reached our stretch goal. The campaign was literally an overnight success. I was overjoyed—I didn't even mind that Lex had woken me up—until I pressed for details and they admitted that Won had posted about the campaign on Instagram. They had called me early so I wouldn't find out on my own.

I hung up. Beside me, Won slept peacefully. I hit him with my pillow.

He came to with a shout. When he saw me, he said, "What the hell?"

"Why did you have to get involved?" I asked. I had explained everything to him and had thought he understood that it was my decision whose name was on the line.

His face immediately softened, slackened. He rubbed the back of his neck.

"So you did know it would piss me off," I said. "Did Lex tell you?"

"It wasn't them."

"I wanted this one thing for myself," I said. Saying it aloud made me realize just how important that had been to me, actually.

Won pulled the covers up to his chin, as if he was embarrassed—or scared.

I tried to calm myself. But I also thought: *Why should I be the one who's careful?*

"I thought you respected me," I said.

"It's not like I did some terrible thing," Won said. "I just made a ten-second video."

My bottom lip curled over my teeth like it was some kind of instinct to keep me from eating him alive. "You did nothing wrong?"

He looked at me like he didn't but was afraid to say so.

"You want me to marry you?"

"Why won't you let me do anything for you?" he asked. He reached for my face. "I see you. You don't have to tough it out alone."

He was throwing my words back at me. I swatted his fingers away.

"Come on, Carrie."

"Don't fucking *come on* me," I said.

"I was just trying to help."

I couldn't get through to his head. His everything-is-fine look was the kind of trap that made me want to make it not fine.

"You're a lifesaver," I said sarcastically. "Thank you for saving me from myself."

He said under his breath that K had asked him to do it.

"Don't you dare use her as an excuse."

He hesitated, then reached for his phone.

"I don't want to see it."

He unlocked the screen and brought up his Instagram.

"I don't want to see it," I said again.

But what I saw was my boss, Top Dog.

Won explained. K had bought him a spy cam, a little pen like he was Korean James Bond or something, and he had emailed my boss for a meeting. He had clipped the pen to his shirt pocket. In the video, Top Dog stomped about, gesticulating as usual. He called Won a fluke and a Chink and told him to fuck off. He said no one wanted to make a show about him. No one would care.

It was a short clip. Probably the rest of it had him cursing me, as he had done when I quit. I had told Won that one day I would get my revenge, knowing I probably wouldn't.

Won's post had thousands of comments. Many called for Top Dog to be fired, though just as many said that Won, in fact, was a fluke and a Chink and should fuck off and stop playing the race card.

"I didn't post anything that would point back to you," Won said. "I just put a link to your Kickstarter."

I didn't say anything. My heart thumped stupidly.

"We wanted to do this for you," he said. "I wanted to do this for you."

I searched for my anger—it was gone.

"Carrie?"

"You don't even give me a ring when you ask me to marry you," I said quietly. "You make it sound like you're just bringing it up out of nowhere. Like it doesn't matter how I answer."

He dropped the blanket and reached down for his pants on the floor. From his pocket, he withdrew a jewelry box. I stared at it with amazement. "You think I didn't get a ring?" he asked. "I just didn't want to scare you off. Or *I* was scared. I didn't want you to reject me."

On his phone, the video looped back, and I heard him called a Chink again. I realized he had risked a lot to post this. He wasn't supposed to remind anyone that he saw color. It could jeopardize his contract, especially after the surgery. His knee was supposed to recover, but there was still some uncertainty. A couple of weeks earlier, the Garden had held a Fortune Cookie Night on which they handed out cookies with a graphic of Won inside, as if his future could be predicted by racism. Which, of course, it could be.

3. CATCH A TIGER BY THE TOE

What Won had done gave me an idea. I borrowed his spy pen and took it with me to Seoul. The network wanted to capitalize on the success of the fortune-teller drama—double-digit ratings on cable!—and bring it back for one special episode of product placement and fan service. Basically, the whole hour would take place in a Subway while various characters ate sandwiches and caught us up on their romances. I didn't have to be there, since the episode wasn't going to stream in America, but I still wanted the PD to direct the basketball show. No—I needed her to. I had come to rely on her, and I had fucked that up by fucking her assistant. I had done a shitty thing and I had to make up for it somehow. Ever since then, our relationship had been all business (in other words: awkward and professional) and it frustrated the hell out of me. She ignored any friend talk.

After asking around at the station, I learned there was a rumor about the PD sleeping her way to better projects, the kind of rumor everyone knows is false but hurts a person anyway. Not a person—a woman. I also learned the rumor about the rumor, since there is always one of those too, that the station chief had started the rumor after the PD refused his advances.

I could believe it, after the meetings about the actor we had to fire. Firing him had significantly bettered the station's image, since it was clear now that he was guilty. The station owed me one, and I was going to collect.

I set up a meeting with the station chief for the day after the filming. I met him in his office in a white blouse unbuttoned to my cleavage, with the camera pen nestled in the chest pocket, and a short black skirt. He shook my hand and thanked me for my hard work. It was a real struggle for him not to stare at my breasts. Somewhat slyly, he mentioned that he was sorry we would no longer be working together, since he had heard I had quit. I said I was thinking about staying and working in Korea, could he give me advice? What could I do to be less American?

His eyes lit up (men love to be asked for advice) and he opened a drawer and took out a bottle of thirty-year-old Glenlivet.

It was so exactly the thing his character would do in a K-drama that it surprised me, like when I made dinner after watching a bunch of "It's a cake" videos and the vegetables I chopped were vegetables.

Some fools embrace whatever cliché offers them the most power.

I let him pour me a drink. As he filled my glass, however, I realized that if I wanted him to incriminate himself, I would have to first put up with the ambiguous stuff. He wouldn't come right out and demand sex. I couldn't even ask him about the rumor directly, since that would point straight back to the PD. I had to catch him being the sleazy asshole he was by experiencing the sleaze myself.

I shuddered. My own hand had shut the door.

"What kind of advice can you offer me?" I asked, trying to make it sound sexy instead of disgusted. It didn't come off.

I was already done for. I had misjudged the game.

He looked away from my chest and put down the bottle,

suspicious. For a moment, I thought he knew about the pen. I stopped myself from looking at it or touching it. But it was simply a time, worldwide, when men were more cautious than usual, because they believed that they were being persecuted.

"I'll go," I said.

He nodded.

I was relieved, and yet I'd done nothing to help the PD. At the door, I said loudly, "Don't hit on your female employees. I'm giving you a friendly warning." I wanted to say something, at least. He sneered, unfazed.

I soon saw why. Instead of attacking him, everyone in the station seemed to attack me with his gaze. I had come out of his office—my own hand had shut the door. This was what the PD was up against. I could escape back to America, but she was stuck here. I realized that sleeping with her assistant and leaving her to clean up the mess must have been like rubbing this fact in her face.

I glared back at the onlookers, but my cheeks burned. I was in danger of blushing. The thing that would really embarrass me would be letting them see me embarrassed. My heart clenched and the blood rose.

"Why are you still standing there?" the chief said. "Get lost."

I was about to hide my face with my hands. Someone stopped my arm.

"Let's go," the PD whispered. She tugged me gently.

She walked us forward, looking ahead, at nothing, like a model on a catwalk. I looked where she looked, and we got out of there together.

4. WATCH OUT FOR DUCKS

On the flight back, I called Ducky. I kept remembering my high school friend jumping off a building. Ducky had told Robert that if he wanted a divorce, he should take everything they owned, even what was only hers; she would "give" it all away, wash her hands of the whole marriage. She had become strangely calm about the changes she was going through, which is one of the signs for suicide.

When I asked how she was doing, Ducky said her therapist had told her she was codependent. "Aren't they supposed to tell you something you don't know? I feel like this asshole keeps repeating the things I tell him and then charges me two hundred dollars for it."

"Do you not like him?" I asked. "Maybe it's time to switch therapists."

"Oh no, I love him. A man who listens to me."

I laughed. I told her I had become an independent producer, meaning I had quit my job. I had realized that the fortune-teller K-drama was the only project I had liked doing in a long time. "Sometimes you know something, but you don't know how to tell yourself it," I said. "I didn't realize what kind of life I had until I realized it wasn't the kind of life I wanted to have."

Ducky said she had wanted a life of no regrets, but the problem with that dream was that once you have one regret, that life is over. One regret and one hundred regrets are the same. "I used to ask myself, before I did anything, if I would regret it on my death bed. I just want to go to Heaven without feeling bad."

This way of decision-making seemed to me a very morbid practice.

"Isn't the nature of Heaven that you won't feel bad?" I said.

She didn't answer.

"My sister, who has cancer, said the other day that it isn't fair how she has to try so hard to live when some people out there just want to die."

I thought I heard Ducky sigh.

"Her only regret is that she won't have more regrets to give."

Crickets.

"Sorry," I said. "Bad jokes are all I have left."

I looked around, nervous that one of the other passengers had heard me.

"You ever shot a gun before?" Ducky asked me.

"Where'd that come from?"

She had been going to the shooting range. "It's very empowering. I might buy one."

"Ducky?"

"You would like it," she said, "if you haven't done it before. You're always so angry. You should join me sometime."

A gun, like regret, always changes the story too late to save it.

"There's nothing wrong with being angry," I said. "Anger tells you that you've been wronged. Whatever you're feeling is valid, I mean. It matters." *Our feelings are pretty smart,* I thought. I didn't want to speak to her, though, in the words of her enemy.

There was an abrupt trio of beeps.

I stared at the airplane phone, wondering whether to call her back. I coiled the cord around my finger, as I used to do as a child, when my parents still kept a landline for overseas calls. Ducky was turning into someone else. Or she was simply letting herself become the person she was afraid of being.

5. KOREAN DINNER

After the PD rescued me from her boss, all seemed to be forgiven. All the tension between us disappeared. It confused me, but I didn't question it. We were texting again! She agreed to direct the basketball K-drama, and I flew her to New York to meet people. It was her first time in America. In meetings, she charmed. Privately, she dished. She wanted to meet Won, who had become some kind of diasporic hero, so I made him join our last dinner. He was glad to be asked: I had asked him for something. I told him not to let it go to his head, but I really loved him. I reserved a private room at a restaurant in Manhattan's K-town—a single street resembling a street in Seoul, neon-lit and filled with Koreans—because after two days, the PD already missed Korean food.

As we ate, Won said it was like the PD and I were the ones in love. She linked arms with me and showed me a photo on her phone that one of the actors from our show had sent her. Won had grown up in LA, so he should have been used to female affection—Korean women often touch each other, unashamed of a woman's body. "What should I call you?" he added. "PD-nim, like Carrie?"

The PD said, with a shy flirtatiousness, that he should call her noona.

I was shocked. "Should I call you unnie then?" I asked, mirroring her tone.

She glared. We had never dropped honorifics.

Won asked how America measured up so far to the PD's expectations. She deboned a fish in five quick movements and placed a piece on each of our spoons. At breakfast, she said, the waiter had talked to her as if she was a baby, and now she was developing an irrational hatred of English, so she didn't know what her expectations were. She said this half like a joke and half like she was going to skin that waiter alive. I wanted to help her. She didn't like anyone speaking informally; she must have hated a teenage boy talking down to her just because he could speak fluently in his first language. Like big fucking deal.

Because of Won, we spoke Konglish. As a kid, Won had refused to learn Korean, because the Korean kids made fun of his American accent; even his younger cousins in Korea laughed at him. His parents were third-generation and could barely speak it either, so they didn't push him, even in K-town. I could speak Korean because my mom had insisted on it after growing up with white adoptive parents, never hearing the language and knowing nothing about Korea except that America had fought a war there. I couldn't imagine what a struggle it had been for her when she first went back to Korea after college, and yet she stayed for six years.

The PD and I spoke to Won in Korean, and he answered back in English, the way he KakaoTalk-ed his relatives. *His* English was excepted from the PD's hatred. If he thought the PD and I acted like we were in love, she looked at *him* like the emoji with hearts for eyes. In Korea, Won's star was still rising: he was an Ivy League grad who even thanked his dad in Korean on TV.

I had helped him practice that sentence in the mirror.

The PD wanted to know if Won watched our show. I hadn't asked him because I didn't want to hear that he didn't watch it—or, maybe worse, that he didn't like it—so I had no idea what he would say. The PD hung on his answer as if she had a bet riding on it.

I was proud of how we had ended the drama, how many tropes we got into the second half of the episode arc, though the PD thought we had gone overboard. The tropes were my favorite part. Once the ghost realizes who Mirae is, it goes through with its plan to get revenge on her by using her body to kill the man she loves. Hwaeen can't fight back because he doesn't want to hurt his beloved. In order to protect Mirae, he breaks up with her and runs away, but the ghost/Mirae hunts him down. When he has nowhere left to hide, he accepts his fate and lets himself be attacked. The ghost, with Mirae's body, beats him to the brink of death. But it is so pleased with its vengeance that its earthly grudge is satisfied. At that, it goes up in black smoke. Mirae comes back to herself and sees what her hands have done. A few nearby ghosts who witnessed the whole thing take pity on her and whisk her away, then lure a passerby, who sees Hwaeen and calls an ambulance. For the next three years, Hwaeen lies in a coma. Mirae trains herself to control her gift, so no ghost will be able to use her again. She befriends good ghosts and vanquishes bad. When Hwaeen finally wakes, she is at his side. Yet here is where the memory loss comes in: he doesn't recognize her. Mirae seeks help from the ghosts she now calls friends. Occasionally, a ghost can't remember its life and doesn't know what it wants and why it hasn't ascended. Mirae helps one of these ghosts recall its memories, and in return, the ghost helps Hwaeen remember his. At last, the two lovers reunite. In the final episode, they marry and start a business together as exorcists.

We played this all tongue-in-cheek and received a lot of praise from hard-core K-drama fans who liked seeing a show take pride in its identity.

"What did you think of the ending?" the PD asked Won at dinner, a clear test.

"I'm still watching," he said. He patted my leg under the table. "It's what I watch during rehab. My PT and I both love it."

The PD practically batted her eyelashes.

I wouldn't find better timing—it's best to apologize to someone when they're in a good mood. I had an apple in my bag for an emergency snack, and I placed it on the table (the words for "apple" and "apology" are homonyms in Korean).

"I'm sorry I fucked your assistant," I said to the PD. "It was out of line."

"What?" Won said.

I explained this was a while ago, before he proposed taking *open relationship* off the table, before I saw the ring.

I had finally figured out why the PD had gotten so upset with me—the real reason had come to me when she complained about the waiter. My one-night stand with her assistant had introduced a kind of English between us, a language the PD didn't want to speak. That was why her comfort returned after rescuing me. I had gone back to speaking a language she understood.

The PD shook her head and called me "babo," affectionately.

We laughed and joked around, insulting one another, having a riotous time, until someone in the adjoining room knocked on the wall and shouted, in English, about the noise.

Once we had finished eating and were on our sixth bottle of soju, the PD said we should hit up New York Korean-style. She was drunk and full of swagger. To me, and probably to Won too, this was the real trial: did we understand what was Korean-style and what wasn't? I thought Korean-style meant *han,* which my mom liked to say was the Korean emotion adoptees understand best: the sadness of generational oppression and yet the will to fight back. It's the emotion that translates easiest to the diaspora.

I remembered the kimchi Won had left outside of Robert Sung's apartment—Robert had asked *us* why someone would leave it there and whether we thought it was racist; Won and I barely held back our laughter—and I told the PD this story. From there, things somehow escalated to playing a game and kimchi-slapping the loser, which was a popular meme on Twitter.

I don't know. We were drunk.

We played the game of wits. In the game, players stand and count off in order. The first person who stands says, "One," the second says, "Two," etc. If two people stand at the same time, they lose. If everyone else counts off, the last person sitting loses. It's really a game for more than three people. We decided to play until only one person lost, so only one person would get kimchi-slapped. If two of us stood at the same time, we started over again. Winning relied on two people being individuals in order to leave a third individual alone.

Of course, we each rushed to be first, so we all lost: we never got past "one." Another knock came from the adjoining room, which only made us laugh louder. We played twelve, thirteen times—until in our joy was also frustration. We were ecstatically annoyed with each other, cackling with exasperation, demanding that someone stand alone and lose. That was what losing was: individualism among companions. That was what death was. I thought of my sister at home with her husband, planning her own funeral. Earlier that night, the PD had asked about K, and I had described K's plan. In reply, the PD said that she had lost a friend to stomach cancer, a man she loved dearly, and after he died, his family took out their grief on his widow. They had a toddler, and his family wanted the child and hired an expensive lawyer to make a case against the mother. The lawyer revealed that the mother had slept with women. Since this was Korea, the mother never saw her kid again. "It's good," the PD said, red-eyed, "that your sister is doing her funeral now. Then she can say exactly what she wants to happen after she dies and can see to it that it does. My friend, he never would have wanted his family to take the baby away from his wife. Your sister will be more at peace this way." Later, Won and I would agree that something about the way she had told the story had made it seem like she was really telling it about herself.

Finally, we decided not to throw kimchi at one of us but to throw it at someone we hated. Won's first thought was the Knicks' owner, who kept stringing him along. We looked up the guy online, but he lived in a giant mansion on Long Island. We needed someone we hated in Manhattan.

That was how we ended up in the garden of the IBM building, our faces hidden by hospital masks, about to toss a quart of kimchi across the street onto the second-floor window of Trump Tower.

Why there? I had worked on a film once about a man who wants nothing and so takes on other people's desires as his. This phenomenon is called mimetic desire. The film depicts an extreme example, but we embrace substitutes all the time. Trump was that substitute for white Americans. What Won made Asian Americans feel was mimetic *wonder*. His story made our own more possible. We loved him because we wanted to love ourselves.

What I mean is, I *was* making a show about him in a way—because I was making my own wonder.

The PD came to her senses first. She asked who would clean the windows. All the kimchi slap would do was make more work for the window washers. We came down from the garden, and Won and I took the kimchi home with us, to eat. I used it for a few pots of soup, but the kimchi was store-bought and tasted like chemicals.

6. LOVING IS AS LOVING DOES

At the end of March, Brit organized a trip to the soup kitchen for the wives and girlfriends of Knicks players. She was their—our—queen bee, due to Powerball!'s status on the team and her own status as an actress. The email string quickly got out of control. The topic was whether or not Brit would still be a "basketball wife" by the end of the season. Everyone knew about her affair, and that knowledge left her position vulnerable (or so I surmised, translating the email string into something I could understand). Some of the other more established partners were rebelling, smelling blood in the water.

I forwarded the string to K, who agreed it was as good as a K-drama. Power was up for grabs. I got so curious about what would happen next that I put the date in my calendar, even though I wondered whether anyone else would show up.

Every single one of them came. As if Brit had known that they would all along, she greeted each woman with a smile and a polite hello. It was a *fuck you* kind of hello. As they arrived, the women all looked around in the same way, unsure of Brit's plan and trying to sniff it out. Brit assigned them jobs she thought might suit them, and the regular volunteers went over what to do.

I was put on serving duty, where the job was simple: give everyone the same amount, keeping resentment low and efficiency high. It felt a little like I was a machine on the production line of goodwill, but that was just the general mood of helplessness I had been stuck in lately. It wasn't anyone's fault.

Everyone awkwardly went to work. None of the other women seemed to expect the work to be so serious, but because Brit took it seriously, they couldn't just brush it off. For Brit, the work was not an opportunity for publicity—she hadn't told the media at all. When some of the other women asked where the reporters were, Brit responded as scornfully and politely as possible. She said, unfortunately, it hadn't crossed her mind that such an outing would be newsworthy. With the regular volunteers, she spoke with an easy familiarity, and they, in turn, treated her like one of their own, not like a potential sponsor or anyone they should impress. It turned out Brit had been volunteering at this location almost every other weekend for the past eight years. We were on her home court.

Once everything was cooked and ready to serve, the doors opened and the first wave entered. The visitors also treated Brit like a childhood buddy. The ones who were obviously most used to the place patted her on the arm or asked about her kids. The whole time, Brit appeared to do nothing to address the email string, yet it felt as if she had answered it in full. I could tell that the others felt the same: confused as to how she was asserting her power, yet certain she was. I had never heard her sound so unaffected, so at ease, as she did in that soup kitchen, like that was the place where she was the least afraid of herself.

We served for about half an hour before Robert Sung appeared. He walked straight past the line waiting for their food. He apologized for being late, kissed Brit on the cheek, and slipped on a pair of plastic gloves.

A few women murmured, and I thought Brit was about to lose the edge. But then the regulars started saying what a handsome young couple they made, how cute Robert was, how helpful and hardworking, how much he doted on her—and no one else could say a thing. What was clear was that Powerball! had never volunteered there; none of the regulars had ever met him. Robert played the part of the perfect gentleman. He watched Brit's every move. He wiped her clean if a tray splattered, lifted away any heavy object she carried, handed her whatever she needed before she had to ask. No one could criticize her openly because she looked so happy, like the criticism wouldn't matter to her. Her happiness swallowed up every attack. Envy clouded some of the other women's faces. Their desire to be in her position established her position once more.

I had to hand it to her. The only hole in her defenses was how willing she was to give up her old life—regardless of whether she knew what she was giving up or not.

7. DYING TO LIVE

K had her funeral in the Korean church our family had gone to for years. We filled the pews. How could we not, after she worked so hard to arrange the flowers and music and Bible readings and even a funeral portrait surrounded by an elaborate display of carnations? On every other row she hung a white bouquet of lilies and roses and gladioli. She spared no expense, left nothing for a second funeral. I couldn't go through another funeral anyway. She even eulogized herself, though it seemed against the spirit of the thing. She wept for her own death.

"I wish she had lived to see all of you here in one place," she said about herself. "It would have made her very happy. The last time we talked, she said, 'This is not a life, just a-live.' She was in so much pain. She couldn't do anything she used to love to do. I asked why she loved the things she loved—going to the movies or a concert, eating out, drinking margaritas, lying on the beach, singing karaoke—wasn't it doing those activities with the people she loved that she loved? Even if she couldn't *do* love, she *had* love. Wasn't that life? I wish she had been able to see that before she died."

She recounted the story of her imaginary friend, the one she had invented when she was seven, too old for it, after we moved towns and left our old school behind. The imaginary friend was exactly like K, except that she could fly and shoot fire from her hands and talk to machines and convince people to do anything she wanted. We used to have a lot of fun together, me and K and imaginary K—even when the two of them would gang up on me and light me on imaginary fire. As K eulogized herself, it was as if she and her friend had switched places. She was the imaginary one now. The real her was dead.

If, until that point, people seemed unsure how seriously to take her, now they wept openly. K raised her head in prayer, and we looked up with her. Did she see her imaginary friend up there, flying around the ceiling and throwing down flames? We were the ones burning up, turning to ash.

"I failed you," K said about herself. "I should have been there for you, and I wasn't."

There was not a dry eye.

In my eulogy, I told the story of how I came to call her K, and how, later on, when I read Kafka for the first time, it seemed as if I had found my sister trapped in his world, trying to understand how she was guilty when she couldn't remember committing a crime. That was the life we lived, I said—that was the prison we occupied—and I had been able to survive it because I had always had her. I said K had been my best friend all my life, though I didn't realize it was so until adulthood. What made me realize, at last, was how, with her, I never felt like I had to be an adult. With her, I still felt the awe of childhood, as if we were always just about to grow up, our dreams still intact. In every production I ever did, I said, my understanding of the characters' love for each other came from the love I felt for my sister (not that I didn't love Won). How could I live in a world without her love for me?

The scene became full-on melodrama. Tears flowed. People

reached for each other's arms. Heartbroken, we filled our hearts. K seemed comforted by all our mourning, which made us mourn more. Afterward, we took a group photo, while she could still be in it. She stood in the center in a black hanbok, beside her husband, who wore an armband over his suit sleeve to designate him as the first bereaved. They held each other. The shutter snapped. We walked away—but they continued to stand there until the pose became their lives. Before we left, K plucked one of the carnations from the frame of her portrait.

On the way to the car, she whispered to me and Fred that she was tired, and we held her body up and helped her walk, trying not to let it show that we were taking steps for her. She told us not to rush to be with her in death, to figure out what we wanted from our lives.

"Don't let anyone kill your wonder," she said, which at first disappointed me, that she would use her "last" words to me to pun on my boyfriend's name—but she meant, she explained later, that to keep our wonder, we had to stop fighting and denying our grief. We had to know how to survive death in order to know how to live.

8. HUMANITY IS HUMANITY'S LAST FRONTIER

After the funeral, we all went to a cousin's Chinese restaurant. K was supposed to eat a few bites six times a day. About half those times, she threw everything back up. If she did get a bite down, she would wrestle with her digestion, then smile and ask Fred to praise her.

The restaurant was as big as a banquet hall and often held events, but K had run out of money to reserve it. Instead, our cousin had held as many tables as we needed. Regular customers ate at the rest of the tables. When we got there, half the room was packed. Won and I and K and Fred and our parents and our three older brothers and their partners sat at one of the large round tables in the center. I hadn't met all of my brothers' partners yet. The newest was a reserved Latino with hearing aids who seemed overwhelmed by our loud Korean family. He was a couple of years older than me. I put Won next to him so they could commiserate. They seemed to get along.

"My cancer friends keep dying," K was saying. "Everyone knows when you die, but no one ever sees anyone die. There's a metaphor, right? Maybe that's why I wanted to do this. I wanted to *see*. What's strange is I still feel like I'll get through all of this."

"You will get through it," Fred said.

"You don't have a choice," Dad said, in typical form. "That's all you can do, is get through this."

"What did he say?" one of the partners asked.

"I said she doesn't have a choice," Dad said in English.

"He said that's all she can do," the oldest brother said.

I put my arm around my sister.

"It hurts when you guys touch me," K said. "I'm just letting you know what I'm going through. It doesn't mean stop. I'm fighting with pain every day. But I'm trying." She took Fred's hand. I wondered if they had finally made a breakthrough, as he didn't change the subject or beg her to eat.

Beside me, Won struggled to explain the ins and outs of the situation to my brother's boyfriend. My brother filled in some of the missing gaps. His boyfriend nodded and sucked down his noodles. He seemed fine with the heat, which made him one of us. We were a jjamppong family. I put some yellow radish on my plate and a piece of tangsooyook on top.

"Hey," someone said loudly a few tables down, "where are their dishes on the menu? You only serve the good stuff to Chinese people?"

We were eating Korean Chinese, which was something these guys probably had never even seen before. They were eating American Chinese, which you couldn't see in Asia.

Suddenly K shouted, "You want cancer? That's what I've got. I've got cancer. You want it?"

A couple of white guys got up, and one said, "Is that the Wonderkid?"

I reached for the scissors. We were all in black. It was obvious we were grieving.

"I'm here for my sister-in-law's funeral," Won said. "No disrespect, but just let us be, okay?"

They started toward us. With the Wonder over, white fans always wanted Won to be grateful they still knew his name, as if their recognition made him exist.

As soon as they got close enough, K threw up all over their shoes.

She targeted their shoes, I mean, even though the doctor had said vomiting was as bad as not eating.

They looked at her then, really looked at her, and maybe they saw she actually did have cancer; she was bone-white and all bone.

"Sorry," one mumbled. They backed away and made their way to the bathroom.

"Shit," our youngest oppa said. "I thought it was going to be a fight. I was ready."

"Stop smiling," my mother said. "It's a funeral."

"Smile," K said. "I want you to smile and think of me throwing up on them."

I got down to help clean the mess.

Later, K held her head in her hands as Mom rubbed her back, and said, "Sorry, Lord," loud enough that it made everyone except Mom stop what we were doing.

"It's okay," Mom said quietly, "your body rejected them. We're here with you. All of us who love you."

It was like the sound fading out in a movie, how quiet we got, until it was just the two of them, together, at the center. They didn't even seem to notice. They knew what to say with each other, how to hold each other's presence—they had a relationship no one else could access. Mom had one with each of us, somehow. I wondered where in her heart she had enough room. I wondered how she could do that, make enough room for all of us but also each of us. What would she do with K's room when K was gone?

It was hard for me to talk.

"I would have lived better if I had really *wanted* to live before,"

K said. "Before cancer, I never thought about living. I wanted so many other things. Now I just want to survive. Why can't I do that?"

From that day on, I always thought of a funeral as a last plea for life.

9. AND AT THE END OF THE STORY IS THE TELLING OF IT

We held the table read for the basketball K-drama in June, after Won's season was over. I'm skipping ahead now. The Knicks had barely made the playoffs. Won's coach had wanted him to play, but risking further injury would have meant risking his contract. His agent told him not to play. I told him not to play. But the media hammered him for it. He had broken the rules of gratitude: as an Asian, he was still supposed to jump at any chance to get on the court. Without him, the Knicks were swept in the first round. Again.

Meanwhile, the PD and I had gone about casting. The American side went smoothly. Most of the Asian American actors we wanted had depressingly free schedules. Many already watched K-drama and had heard about the project. I had grown up with K-drama as something Koreans did in private and didn't tell anyone else about, so I was forever amazed that it was now a thing. The Korean actors were harder to cast. Their schedules were packed. An American production excited them, but they were cautious. It hurt our case that I had changed production companies. (I had gone back to the company my college friends still ran.) A smaller company made them wary. The PD and I had to sell the Korean actors on our success in Korea—which meant the ratings for the fortune-teller drama.

Finally, when all those schedules aligned, we flew the Americans to Seoul to meet the Koreans. We were preproducing every episode, so everything was written and ready to film—first the scenes in Korea and then the scenes in America. We had doubled the crowdfunding money with support from a studio and were flush with cash. Watching the Korean American actress who never got a starring role trade quips with the Korean A-lister who headlined everything he did, I couldn't look away. It added a natural dynamic to her role as a sportswriter from America sent to Korea on a lesser assignment, discriminated against for her sex and race, and his role as a superstar Korean basketball player recognized everywhere he goes in Seoul. By the end of the second episode, she writes her first big story exposing the star for betting on and throwing an important playoff game. This story makes her career and ends his. What she doesn't know is that he only bet on the game because his brother's secret daughter, the child of an affair, ran off with her mother to America and promptly got in a car accident. The child had emergency surgery and fell into a coma. The mother died on impact. Without American insurance, the bills were astronomical, but it was too dangerous to transport her back to Korea. She had to stay. To pay her bills, the star used up all his savings *plus* the money for throwing the game. He even took out a loan to give her mother a funeral, since his brother was afraid to reveal his affair by paying for anything. After the write-up, the star gets kicked out of the KBL and loses everything to his debtors. He goes to his brother for help, since he doesn't want to worry his parents. Even after all he has done and given up for his brother, his brother turns him away. Abandoned and broke, and still trying to hide it from his parents, the star camps outside the sportswriter's apartment building. Once in the morning and once at night, he tries to convince her to write something on his behalf. Each time, they talk, they bicker, they argue, they start to empathize. They feel strangely let down when they don't see each other. In episode four, one of the star's fans breaks into the sportswriter's apartment while she is out. When she gets home, he ties her up, blames her for ruining the star's career, and tells her everything she doesn't yet know about the star's sob story. Finally, he goes for her throat. Just as she is about to pass out, the star rushes in, and the episode ends.

SPORTSWRITER

Why don't you just get a new job?

STAR

What can I do? All I know how to do is shoot a ball through a hoop. I spent my whole life perfecting that one thing, and without it, I'm going mad.

SPORTSWRITER

If you were a woman, you would get death threats, and fans of both teams would come after you. You just lost your job. You can go back to your parents if you choose. Your life isn't ruined—you have a whole support system. What do you want from me? You want an article about how a disgraced star is now stalking the journalist who exposed him? No one would care. You're not a story anymore.

STAR

You think I *chose* to be here? I didn't. It wasn't a choice. I'm here because of your story. That's who I am now, and you're responsible. You have to take responsibility.

SPORTSWRITER

Open a chicken place or something. Go back and bother your family.

STAR

(thinking about his brother)

I don't have anyone to bother but you.

SPORTSWRITER

(after some hesitation)

I had to leave my entire family to come here. Because I couldn't go any further as an Asian American woman sportswriter. You have no idea what it's like to grow up idolizing athletes, people like you, wanting to be a part of their sport, working your way through college, being harassed by male colleagues and editors, only to get sent out of the country on assignment. And still, after all that, I was excited to meet you. I was excited to meet you, and you turned out to be a cheater. *I'm* the one who has only this one thing left that I can do—and I don't even know if I like it anymore. *I'm* the one going mad.

STAR

(stepping closer, startling both of them)

I just want my life back.

SPORTSWRITER

I just want my own life.

In that room around that table, we all breathed deeply, feeling the chemistry, the kind that means there will be life in the show. A good table read stirs everyone's imagination. Like falling in love, you envision the show in its most perfect form—and that vision is collective. It's as if each person brings a flower and, by looking around at all the flowers other people brought, you picture the entire field. The collectivity is the most romantic part. It isn't one person's perfect vision, it's the many visions of perfection that in reality could never all be fulfilled but that, until they are real, are all still possible.

I could see my version clearly now, each character flustered by the heat of the other's body, confused by the sympathy they feel, since they're supposed to be enemies, voices trembling with anger and vulnerability. Each notes the other's pain but thinks the other doesn't notice theirs.

Near the end of the read, my phone buzzed—Won calling from New York. I had told him my schedule ahead of time, so the call had to be important. We took a short break. I FaceTimed Won, who looked stricken, struck, his face red and his eyes sunken. He said the Knicks had refused to match Houston's offer — after the owner had told him to go out and get an offer so they could match it. "I don't know what to do," he said. "They completely fucked me. They want it to look like I chose to leave New York. What are we going to do?"

The voices of the characters I had created still rang in my ears. *I didn't choose to live on my own,* they were saying, *I am on my own because I chose life.* That's how they end up together too: they choose each other because they choose to live.

"Fuck the Knicks," I said. "Show them your power. Get free."

Won coughed as if I had startled him.

"Let's get married," I said. "You got a contract. Congratulations."

10. A GOOD K-DRAMA IS ALWAYS A CAKE

Much later, long after the basketball K-drama aired, a fan emailed me that she had done some hard looking to find not the actors or director of the show, but the person who had come up with the original idea. She said she had found online that I was married to Won, and she remembered those seven wins as the time in her life she most loved being an American, before America became a climate nightmare and Nazi-sympathizers and government-mandated lockdown. The show also meant something to her personally. She was an adoptee, and she had searched for years for her Korean family, and in the end, she had found her birth mother, who had left her birth father and then married and had three kids with her husband. At first, her birth mother refused to see her. She had to wait five years, from before the drama aired to long after, before she was finally able to see her Korean mother again. On the flight over, she was so angry that she convinced herself that it was a mistake to go there, that it would have been better to have never searched at all. But when she landed, her birth mother was there with her birth father and his entire family. In shaky English, her birth mother apologized to her and said she had spent the past few years finalizing her divorce from her husband and her separation from their kids, because they refused to accept her as the mother of another child, one she had given up for adoption. She had had to lose everything, she said, to understand how that child must have felt, and then she had started English lessons and found the birth father, and together they had made a plan.

The fan who wrote to me, she said that because she had seen the drama and found out about me and Won and then even about my mom being adopted, she had managed the strength to reunite with her Korean mother, and even convinced her adoptive parents to move to Seoul for six months so they could all be together. At the end of the note, she said she was sorry, because she had watched the show for free, through someone's pirated YouTube channel, but she hoped I might understand and forgive her. Which I did, of course, because what is forgiveness in the face of such a wondrous life?

PART SIX
WON

I. A JOKE ABOUT WONDER, CONTINUED

Let me rewind here. I'm taking the story back now, back to the funeral that Carrie's sister held for herself. That night, I got caught up in the courage she had, to stare down her own death. I texted Sung about the rest of his basketball joke. What happens next? I asked. What happens after they want to see the size of the AsAm baller's dick?

Ball or dick, Sung texted back, ignoring my sincerity. I regretted asking him.

2. TO WHOM DOES A PERSON BELONG

It was only a few days after the funeral, at the beginning of April, that Robert Sung finally acted on his threat. At that time, my knee was still injured; we were maybe three-quarters of the way through the regular season. That morning, I was watching tape of myself on the laptop when Carrie rushed in and switched on ESPN. At first, I thought she wanted me to get mad with her at how they had mixed up Sung and me on national TV—they had put my headshot on the screen just above his name and a couple of tweets from his account—but that was only the beginning.

Sung's tweets implied that Powerball! was throwing games. The Knicks were on the playoff bubble, and if they stopped trying to get in and lost instead, they would get a better draft pick. The top three prospects in the draft were all point guards—so if they could get a good-enough pick, the position they would replace was mine.

In other words, it looked like Powerball! was losing games in order to get rid of me and start next season with a new point guard.

"Didn't think the fucker would go that far," Carrie said. I thought she was talking about Powerball!, until she added, "He really thinks a scandal will get Brit to fall out of love with Paul Burton?"

Then I understood: It was the first time in Sung's career that he had ever criticized Powerball! To do so now meant that he was purposefully trying to hurt PB, either by lying or by revealing a secret. Either way, the trust between them was over. Their relationship would never recover from this.

I remembered how Sung had said he would "bury" Powerball! Had he meant this?

"Sung couldn't make up something this huge," I said to Carrie, "could he? The truth will come out sooner or later. He'd be shooting himself in the bridge. He'd be burning his foot."

Carrie's nose wrinkled. "So, what, you think Paul Burton hates you so much that he would miss the playoffs?"

"Powerball! doesn't hate me," I said, my mouth dry. "He hates losing."

"Exactly. You mix up idioms when you're scared."

I didn't think that was true, but I wasn't sure.

I stood up for a glass of water and didn't get far. I couldn't stop staring at the TV. Something about my photo attached to Sung's tweets bothered me even more than your usual microaggression. It was more than just another case of all-Asians-look-the-same. It was worse somehow.

I stared until I figured it out.

My photo there made it look like *I* was the one accusing Powerball!, like I was trying to get revenge on him for injuring me.

"Everyone's going to think I'm Sung's source," I said. "I've got to tell PB before he gets the wrong idea. Like two Koreans against a Black dude. Like so much for solidarity."

"Jagiya," Carrie said, a term of endearment she never used.

"They're all going to blame me."

"That's their racism," Carrie said, "not ours."

3. PUBLIC RELATIONS

Just as Carrie predicted, I couldn't stop the media from going after me. But I wanted to do something to show Powerball! my loyalty. I couldn't make a statement that I was not Sung's source, since he had already said so and denying it would make it seem like there was more to deny. I had to do something to counter the rumors without acknowledging their existence. I figured it would be best to talk to Powerball! directly and take a photo or record a video together to show our support for each other. There was nothing else I could do except stay away from Sung until people knew the truth.

I worried that Powerball! wouldn't want to see me, but when I texted him about stopping by, all he said was that he might have the kids. Brit was supposed to leave them for the weekend—they were trying a separation, seeing what it would be like to split custody, even if, in reality, Powerball! had to hire a sitter. The season left little time for families. I had trouble enough finding time to go on a date with Carrie.

Powerball!'s condo took up the entire top floor of a building in Chelsea. I checked in with the doorman and took the private elevator in the back of the building. Powerball! met me at the doors. He was in sweats. The kids weren't there. Brit was running late. He was carb-loading for the game that night, frustrated, and he offered me some pasta. I wanted booze or a joint, since I wasn't playing, but he didn't want Brit to smell anything—he even lit these high-end candles—so I watched him eat alone. The condo sparkled, full of light, huge and open and immaculately decorated. It looked like he had added furniture since the last time I had been there, when we just hung out and got high, like getting high with your mayor. There's a level of millionaire that looks nothing like the middle class. A private chef had cooked his pasta and left before I got there.

I told Powerball! I didn't know anything about Sung's tweet, but he didn't even care. The accusation that he was cheating seemed to mean nothing to him. He asked if I knew whether Brit had bought a place of her own or was living with Sung—had Sung said anything about *that*? All I knew was that Ducky had moved out and gone back to Connecticut to live with her mom.

"You're walking okay, I see," Powerball! said, which was his way of asking how my recovery was going.

"I might be able to get back on court by the playoffs," I said. "If we get in."

He said I shouldn't rush it. Then he asked about Carrie—were she and Brit still in touch? I realized it had taken him an effort to stop talking about Brit long enough to ask about my injury. I felt oddly grateful.

"She must be worried about me, right?" he asked.

I didn't follow.

"Brit, I mean. You even listening? She'd worry, right, that I might get in trouble with the league? With the law?"

He thought that the accusation would backfire, that Brit would feel sorry for him and recognize that she still loved him, her husband and the father of their children. Any minute now, was his expectation, Brit would ascend the elevator and continue their old life.

It was messed-up, lovesick reasoning. On the other hand, he harbored no suspicions of me. I didn't factor into his thoughts either way. To Powerball!, all this was just a fight between him and Robert Sung.

I felt sure again that he had injured me not out of malice but out of having a lot of other things on his mind.

I was about to excuse myself when Brit came over the intercom. She didn't have keys anymore.

Brit was dressed up, as if the extra effort was why she was late—her face shone, her jewelry twinkled, her hair hung perfectly over one shoulder—but the jury was still out on whether it was for Powerball! The kids rushed past their dad to the TV without saying hello. I waved awkwardly.

"God, Won," Brit said. "What are you even doing here? Give us a moment, yeah?"

"Dad," one of the kids shouted. "Come play."

"I was just heading out," I said.

Powerball! stopped me. "Can't you go shoot aliens with the kids?" he asked. "We got stuff to talk about. Keep them busy for a little while? Then we can do the photo thing or whatever."

I hadn't thought he'd heard me.

Brit scowled. She looked like she was going to hand me my coat herself.

I sat with the kids, who knew me vaguely, and they walked me through choosing a character. At the same time, I tried to eavesdrop on their parents. The game took place in the ruins of some kind of spaceship, which the kids said wasn't ours. Apparently, we were the ones who had shot it down. We seemed to be colonizing the aliens' planet. Reluctantly, I shot aliens with them until the ground ran green with blood. They hollered eagerly for murder.

"Wow, you're really good at killing," the youngest boy told me.

"Thanks?"

"How'd you get so good at it?"

When I looked around, Powerball! and Brit were gone. They must have stepped into a room.

"Whoops, now you're dead," said the oldest boy as he shot me in the back.

He shot his siblings in the back too. They whined that we were supposed to be a team.

"Let's chill out on the 'killing' and 'dead' language," I said.

"Why? It's not like we're saying 'fuck' or 'shit.'"

"Maybe I should check on your parents." I put down the controller.

The oldest shot me again since I wasn't moving. I mean, he shot my avatar.

"See?" the youngest said. "He always does that."

"They're just fucking," the oldest said, emotionless. He began doing something to my dead body. "Why are your ears turning red? What are you, a baby?"

That's when the shouting started. It wasn't good shouting. The kids stopped annoying each other and grew quiet. In a moment, the door flung open. The middle kid rubbed his stomach, rubbed, rubbed. Then Brit ran out of the bedroom, her dress in disarray, grabbed her coat, and left.

From the boys came a total, eerie silence. The little girl cried.

Powerball! came out sighing, sat down, and pulled his daughter onto his lap. I couldn't tell how he felt. He started killing the aliens not like he was angry at them, but like nothing was wrong with them except that they were aliens. He hugged his boys and told them not to shoot each other, and they listened. The middle boy pushed the girl out of their dad's lap and climbed in himself. Powerball! pulled a snack out of somewhere and gave it to the girl before she could retaliate. All was calm, except in the game. In the game, Powerball! organized them into a little killing machine, in sync and working together. I had never seen anything like it.

"How much ammo you got?" he asked the boy on his lap. "Add that to what Sonny's got. How much ammo between you two? Sonny, tell him how much."

I put my controller down. They were engrossed, cooperative, a killer unit of four. I wondered if anyone else on the team had seen Powerball! be a dad like this, providing comfort and stability in the aftermath of discomfort and instability. I felt let in on a secret... the secret that this was his normal life and his secret life was ball.

I wasn't actually that surprised. I wished it did surprise me—that he felt he had to hide this part of his life from the rest of the world—but it didn't. It was like the time my sisters and I brought home a sick bird and almost forgot it didn't belong to us but to the sky. When it flew away, it became itself. I wanted to know more about this side of Powerball! I felt guilty for thinking of him the way people thought of me now, like what they saw on the court was who I was. I wondered what he and Brit had talked about. After all their years together, could she not believe him? Did *she* think he was throwing games? Sadness radiated off him as he murdered extraterrestrials. After a while, we took a photo together and even a video of me and him and his kids on a rampage. He asked his kids whether I could post it online and only let me put it up once they agreed.

4. THE NATURE OF DREAMS

That night, after my visit to Powerball!'s condo, I dreamed that I was back in my childhood home and my mom was alive and everyone was maybe twenty years younger, except for me. I was in my Knicks jersey, late for a game. I had to leave, but I wanted a proper goodbye first. I wanted to hear them say goodbye to me. No one would do this for me. Finally, I screamed that I was late and could not miss the game, that my future depended on it, that everyone was waiting to see me fail, and my family stopped what they were doing and gathered around me in surprise. They opened their arms to me. And yet when I tried to go to my mother, my father, my sisters, each as they used to be, I couldn't seem to cross the years between us. I mean I kept moving toward them, and they didn't move at all, and I never reached them. I knew I had to give up and get to the game, I just needed to reach one of them, once, before I left. If I didn't, I would lose them all forever.

I woke without reaching either my mom's arms or the game. For a while, I lay beside Carrie and tried to dream again. In real life, when I remembered my mom's face, I could recall it only as it looked in photos—specific photos of things we had done together. I couldn't seem to recall her doing those things, moving around, changing her expression, just the moment she was captured on film. Why was that? In my dream, she was alive, spontaneous, real. Maybe we never really know another person if we know them only in reality. I wondered what Carrie's dreams looked like, what world she lived in when she was free to make it up. On the other hand, she was constantly showing that world to people, on-screen. She wasn't hiding anything.

I felt anxious, suffocated. I coughed, and Carrie stretched her arm across my chest and stroked my opposite cheek. "You were dreaming," she said. "It's okay. It's okay." The warmth of her palm calmed me. When I looked over, her eyes were shut tight. She was still asleep, as if her spirit had reached through her dream to touch me.

5. A JURY OF PEERS

In the pregame shootaround, I made my first ten shots, and make by make, I relaxed. I wasn't supposed to be shooting—the shot coach said it would screw up my release to overcompensate for one leg—but I needed to see the ball go through the hoop. Back in the locker room, my teammates eyed me, like maybe on top of being Sung's spy, I was actually fine and only pretending my knee still hurt. The cheating accusation weighed on everyone.

So much seemed to ride on how the game would go. It was pretty clear that the season was over, that the Knicks *would* be better off tanking for a better pick, but now we had to play to win. No one wanted to doubt Powerball!'s integrity, or at least admit they doubted it. Instead, they teased him that he wasn't doing enough to lose, that he was still playing too good. Usually, when the team knew something was bunk, spin, we would talk about it in the open like that. If the team believed a rumor, no one said a word. That was how it was with Sung and Brit, which everyone knew about but no one ever mentioned. Maybe the team would put their trust in PB one last time. Sometimes you have to *choose* what to believe in. Sung was off the media list for the game, but he hadn't complained. As far as I knew, he had accepted that no one in the organization wanted him around anymore. He must have known what would happen if he went after the Knicks' marquee player. He had sent me a couple of texts apologizing for not warning me ahead of time and asking how PB was. I didn't respond.

Powerball! shed the teasing like his old self. He talked shit back, told the guys to watch what happened on the court. His eyes had their old fire. He was locked in. And the team responded—the energy in the room heated up. You could literally feel the temp rise. Something was going to happen.

Whatever it was, I was ready. Ever since I came back from All-Star Weekend angry and promptly injured myself on Powerball!'s foot, the guys had distanced themselves from me. Sung's tweets had only made things worse. Even the video I had taken with PB and his kids made no difference. Now, however, as Powerball! pumped them up, their attitude toward me was already shifting. They pulled me into their jokes. The team dynamic always started with him.

Near the end of the Wonder, when the buzzer had sounded on my seventh win in a row, Powerball! had been the first to reach me. He had leapt off the bench and chest-bumped me so hard I ended up on my ass. Since then, only two months had passed.

Right before tip-off, I caught Powerball! staring off at Brit, who sat four rows behind the bench. She refused to look back. He furrowed his brows; he looked wild to prove something. The whistle blew and the ball went up, and when it came down, it flew straight to him. *Okay,* I thought. *Let's go*... But the first thing he did was turn it over. He threw a bad pass into the stands. On the next play, he reached in and fouled. Then he bricked an off-kilter shot. He jumped for a pass and missed, leaving his man free. I didn't know what he was doing. Coach called a time-out and shouted at him. All PB did was gaze at Brit. As soon as play started again, he dribbled the ball off his foot. I could see the reports already, confirming everyone's worst suspicions. For the first time in his career, the crowd booed him.

Yet he was undisturbed. He continued to play like he wanted their hatred. He wasn't upset when he missed a shot or got beat on defense—things that used to upset him. He seemed to barely hold back a smile. He kept looking at Brit, as if to say, *See?* Maybe I read too much into those looks, but it seemed almost like he was throwing the game just to show Brit that Sung could not intimidate him. He didn't need to prove himself to Robert Sung. In fact, as time went on, I felt even surer. The obvious way he was throwing the game made it clear that he had never thrown a game before. I saw the team realize this too—that if he had really wanted to lose, he could have played far worse. Something relaxed in their faces. They knew that he was clean, unimpeachable. In a word: back.

Brit, though, did not seem to know this, even after all of their years together. Her lips drooped, and she rubbed the back of her neck, disgusted. Finally, she booed along with the crowd. She didn't get him. She couldn't have booed if she did. He was trying to show us all that he was always loyal to the game. He was more faithful and committed than anyone. He had dedicated his life to ball, and still, somehow, we had forgotten this fact. We had forgotten how much he gave to the game, and now it was clear as day. It was clear just how remarkable that gift was, just how rare, just how pitiful and awe-inspiring and marketable. Without that gift, the game was a chore to watch.

As the rest of the team saw what was going on, they seemed to level up their game to balance out Powerball!'s downgrade. I called louder from the bench, wishing I could be out there. They played shorthanded, essentially four on five. At the half, we were down twelve. We could have been down thirty.

In the second half, it was clear to everyone what the team was doing: they were giving him another chance.

Coming out of the half, Powerball! was still, steel. He demanded the ball off our first inbounds pass and took it down the other end and dunked on a poor unsuspecting opponent who had been lured into thinking he was having a purposeful off night. "Poster," I heard the bench whisper. "There he is." I stopped myself from turning and looking back at Brit. For some reason, I knew he wouldn't want me to. This was just between them. The rest of the court—the other team, even our team—all seemed to make way for him, as it always did, until only Brit remained.

Powerball! took the next pass down into the post and hit a fade-away bank. Then an outlet three. Then another poster dunk. By the end of the third, we were up five. We were going to blow Utah out. He was two assists from a triple-double. The team whooped and slapped each other's asses. Powerball! had made his statement clearly—that he could throw a game if he wanted to, and also that he did not, and that he could win a game if he had to, if he wasn't allowed to take a break like other people.

After that game, I would call Sung's boss at ESPN and tell him that Powerball! and I both wanted Sung off the team. He had crossed a line as a journalist; he had crossed a line as a friend; and he had crossed a line as an Asian American, trying to turn me and Powerball! against each other. I would go on TV and defend Powerball!, and Sung would get transferred to Houston.

But to my surprise, Brit would move with Sung. She would leave Powerball! for good.

At the end of the game, when I looked back at her, at last, Brit was cheering from the aisle, having walked down to just above our bench. She smiled at me. It was a small acknowledgment of the mutual awe and love we all experienced, at that moment, for her husband. I was sure then that Robert Sung was lost. I never guessed that the collective feeling in that arena would be, to her, only more damning evidence that she meant less to her husband than basketball.

6. A SERIES OF FATES

To end: a series of fates. Funny how time proved Carrie right that fate is the only way to end a story truly. Who could have predicted how everything turned out? No one but the fortune-teller from her K-drama.

The first fate was Carrie's sister's, who, with maybe three months left to live, qualified for a new clinical trial, some kind of targeted therapy that matched the proteins in her DNA—I got the doctor talk secondhand—and in two weeks, the cancer was reduced by half. Life was possible again; she was going to live. The whole family was ecstatic, overwhelmed with hope in the way you could be only after losing all hope.

It was perfect timing to take Carrie out and convince her that I would be there for her forever. She could once again think about tomorrows. I planned the kind of date that happens on TV. I dropped a few games' pay on a helicopter ride and a necklace with our names on it. I wanted to surprise her, and she'd already seen the ring.

It was more money than I ever handed over in my life—but I was still banking on a contract. The thing with Sung had been cleared up. My knee was recovering well. And since Powerball! had led the team back into the playoff race, a lottery pick—and a new point guard—was out of the picture. I was the best point guard the Knicks could get, plus they knew the millions they could make off me. The owner told my agent that they would match any offer I got on the market.

We were still underestimating racism.

Carrie dressed up for our date in a black dress with black tights and a tan trench coat and even the rare appearance of heels. It was the middle of April, the snow gone, global warming in high effect—but still too cold to look that sexy. I thanked her for her sacrifice. She laughed and said I looked good myself: I wore a white dinner jacket with black slacks and shoes. A limo picked us up, and as we neared the helipad, I pulled out a sleep mask. I planned to tie the string at the back of Carrie's head. When she tensed, I said, "I'm not trying to do weird sex stuff to you," and got embarrassed. She tapped one of the jewelry boxes in my pocket. "Look at that," she said, "you're already hard. What exactly do you plan to give me?" I put the mask away.

The helicopter turned out to be a mistake. We couldn't really hear each other. Only one channel on our headsets worked and we had to share it with the pilot. Carrie clamped her lips tight, and I thought she was disappointed. But when she couldn't hold back any longer, a laugh escaped her. She said that she had once suggested a helicopter date for a romantic comedy and the director had sneered and said there was no romance in talking through headsets as rotor blades whirred overhead.

"I guess he was right and I can let go of that grudge now," she said. "Thank you for that."

"You're welcome," I said sourly.

"Come on. Thank you for making me laugh."

Her laugh *was* nice to hear after how dire things had gotten with her sister.

She peered down at the city below and said, “I feel so alive. How fucking bougie are we right now?”

The Garden resembled a volume knob set in the grid of the city, like I could reach down with God’s hand and lower the sound of the world.

“We are alive,” I said.

“We’re alive,” she said.

“We made it,” I said. “The American dream: looking down on everyone else.”

In college, my teammates and I had bragged that we would get our names in the rafters of the Garden; we could talk big because none of us really believed we would.

I reached in my pocket for the jewelry boxes.

In a second, Carrie went from laughing to crying. Her makeup washed out and black eyes appeared under her thumbs as she brushed away her tears.

“We made it,” she said. “We’re alive.”

My headset crackled.

“Everything okay?” the pilot asked. “Usually, no one cries.”

“Man, I’m trying to propose here,” I said.

I dug the mask out of my jacket pocket and handed it to Carrie to wipe her tears. She tied it over her eyes instead. “Okay,” she said. “You can do weird sex stuff to me now.”

“Um,” the pilot said.

I took off my headset.

I lifted the necklace to her throat and fastened the clasp. She fingered the gold links and the second heart beside her chest. Still blindfolded, she reached for my cheek, she touched my ear. She pushed her mic away and moved her mouth to my skin. “Just how much,” she whispered, “do you think we can freak this fucker out?”

7. THE FATES OF POWERBALL! AND ROBERT SUNG

The relationship between Powerball! and Sung could never be salvaged. Two things happened right before the playoffs. We played our final regular-season game in Houston, which was where Sung had been reassigned. Brit had taken the three kids and moved in with him, though she flew them back and forth once a week to see their dad. I was still stunned by how wrong I had been about her and Powerball! Carrie explained that Brit was *never* that into ball, she had simply supported her superstar husband and felt unsupported in turn. Once again, I had mistaken my feelings as other people's feelings. It was a lesson I needed to learn, about which master empathy served, who empathy rewarded.

The first thing happened at 3:16 a.m. on the day of our final game—I noted the biblicality—which was when Coach called and woke me up in my hotel room. He had never done that before, so I pulled myself together. "Go and see him," he said, without saying who *him* was. His voice was strained, like he hadn't slept all night. "Fucking asshole. Maybe you can snap him out of it. I don't get why he listens to you, but he does."

"Powerball!?" I said.

"Hurry up," he said. "This game has my ass on the line." He hung up.

I called the front desk and asked if anyone ever prank-called. They said they had just put through a call from Coach's room. I was not dreaming. It wasn't a joke, it was just fucked up and high school.

Powerball! opened his door in his airplane clothes. He stank of sweat and something that reminded me vaguely of rust. He had the lights off and said he didn't want them on, they hurt his eyes. He didn't offer me a seat. He sank into the armchair. The curtains stood open at least. Light came in from the city outside.

Since I was already there, I asked him what was going on. I got the feeling that he had been crying and/or doing hard drugs.

"Give me a break," he said.

"A break from what?" I asked. "You got to tell me what first." How did anyone ever understand anyone else when people so rarely explain themselves? Maybe to most people, understanding is beside the point.

"I don't see what she sees in him," he said with a whine that sounded more like a bird than a role model.

"Get it together," I said, wishing to hold on to my youth.

"Sorry I fucked up the All-Star Game. You didn't deserve that."

If the lights had been on, he would have seen my jaw drop.

"Wasn't really about you anyway," he said, and asked for some aspirin.

"Why *did* you turn everyone against me like that?" I asked, unable to stop myself.

He searched my face—at least, I imagined he did—as if something in it would determine how he should answer, or even whether he had an answer in the first place.

"Never mind," I said. "I don't want to know."

"Sung thinks he's you," Powerball! whined. "He thinks if you fuck whoever you want, he can fuck whoever he wants, he can fuck my wife. He thinks I'm the only reason he's not you, I'm the only reason he's not with Brit, when he just has no talent. And then I look over and you're trying to get with some Korean chick like you think you made it..."

"Fuck you," I said. I tried to calm my breathing. "What a fucking active imagination."

He scoffed.

"I made it," I said. "I definitely made it. Otherwise, why stick your foot under me?"

"Motherfucker," he said. "You know I didn't do that."

I wanted to forget how I had idolized him—but I couldn't. I knew how tired he was, how broken, how close to losing his love for the game.

"Just go to sleep and let's make the playoffs," I said.

"You got nothing to do with that."

"Thanks to you."

He turned away.

"Thanks to you," I repeated.

He didn't say anything else.

The next day, Powerball! was late to the pregame shootaround. "What'd you do to him?" Coach asked me, like it was my fault. I had to bite my tongue to keep from cursing him out.

Only five minutes passed, but Powerball! was never late. The guys muttered to each other and glanced at me in punctuation.

"Go on," I said. "Out with it." I was too worked up to care.

The center we called Tree looked down at me suspiciously. "You don't know?" he said. "Aren't you tight with PB?"

"What about him?" I asked.

Tree said that the afternoon before, Powerball! had found out where Sung lived in Houston and gone for a fight. He broke Sung's nose and a couple of ribs, in front of Brit and the kids.

Tree arched his eyebrows as if he expected me to run off at this news—to go to one of them, I guess, though I didn't know which one he thought that was.

"How bad?" I asked.

"Bad." Apparently, Powerball! had stopped after a few swings and tried to leave, but Sung kept coming for more, wanting to get a punch in. "That's how the little guy got his ribs broke," Tree said.

I winced at that "little guy"—though the difference was indeed fifty pounds or more.

Why had Sung, who was a coward, continued to get up? I had to hand it to him. He would at least sacrifice himself for the person he really loved. Whether that meant protecting Brit or—maybe—accepting his punishment from Powerball!

"Where'd you hear that?" one of the others asked.

"You know. Team security, rumor mill, whatever. It'll get covered up by tomorrow like PB's other bullshit."

At that point, Powerball! came in and they went to him as if nothing had happened.

I was the one left there, feeling like no one was sincerely on his side. He had to be so lonely. Somehow, we had ended up each other's only real friends on the team. I hadn't noticed because of my problem of projecting my feelings onto everyone else. I was the one who loved Powerball!—me personally, not the rest of the team. The guys just wanted to win, which Powerball! could do for them. For the first time, I considered the possibility that Sung's betrayal was the one that hurt Powerball! the most, not actually his wife's. In a way, Robert Sung had been his oldest and closest friend.

What all Powerball!'s other bullshit was, I never found out.

8. THE FATE OF DUCKY SUNG

The second thing that happened, happened to Ducky. She had moved back to her childhood home and cut off contact with Sung and everyone else in New York. So it wasn't until the Knicks had dropped out of the playoffs that Carrie and I finally heard the news of her death.

"I can't believe she really killed herself," I said.

Carrie said it wasn't suicide. She kept refreshing her email in shock.

What happened wasn't anything anyone could have predicted. Ducky was hit by a bicycle. It was like fate had swooped down and taken her in exchange for Carrie's sister, like the universe had to balance out. We couldn't get over it. The biker was completely fine. Even the bicycle was barely worse for wear; it had started in terrible shape and came out with no additional damage, only bloodied and cursed.

Ducky had been out for a walk in her old neighborhood, when a teenager on a flea-market bike came racing at her. The biker bailed. The bike skidded toward her. As Ducky tried to jump out of the way, she twisted her body and somehow fell on top of it. It was the handlebar that killed her. It was missing a grip and was bare and rusted into a fatal instrument. All this would come up later, in the trial, how unbelievable the coincidence was, the kind of thing that could happen only in real life (or K-drama), how much the teenager could really be blamed. When Ducky fell, her neck landed full force on the exposed metal tube, which impaled her.

It was totally, absolutely ridiculous. Which was why we had to believe every word.

When Carrie told her sister, K said: "I survived cancer for *this*? For this kind of world? What a joke!" She took it back quickly and blessed herself.

Carrie and I went to the funeral together. I had thought K's funeral was morbid, but Ducky's was far worse. Instead of talking about how she had lived, all anyone could talk about was the brutal way she had died. They whispered about her separation and the unlikely details of her accident, though everyone must have already known. I kept thinking there was no frame of reference for her death—that was why it overshadowed her life. Of course, I didn't say this. I found Sung and patted his sweaty hand, since he actually did seem regretful and since nearly everyone else avoided him and since death was not the time to be alone, and Carrie and I placed a lily on the coffin and said a prayer for Ducky's parents, that they would not be too bitter at how their beloved daughter was remembered.

9. THE FATE OF FATE

That off-season was the last time I saw Robert Sung. He returned to New York for the summer, since Brit wanted to feel out modeling opportunities and the kids wanted to see their dad. Apart from Ducky's funeral, Sung and I were still not talking. He had protected himself from the possible legal trouble of his tweets by refusing to reveal his source, which made it look like he was the messenger and his source was the one to kill. If anyone believed him, then they still believed that source was me. Soon it was revealed that Powerball! and I had demanded his transfer to another team's beat. After that, I didn't hear from Sung for a while.

Then he broke the news that Houston had offered me thirty million guaranteed over three years, more money than I could imagine. The Knicks had promised to match, and my agent was trying to get them to honor that promise, but in our meetings, they lowballed. Once Sung went public with their promise and Houston's higher offer, they were forced to stop. They didn't want anyone to know how little they valued me.

It made me wonder whether Sung wanted to mend things between us. He'd backed the Knicks into a corner. My agent said we should thank him.

Yet the actual result was that the Knicks refused to officially make an offer at all. To pay what I was worth, they would have to pay a luxury tax for passing the salary cap, and though they made tens of millions of dollars off Wonder merchandise, the owner said they weren't willing to "take another chance" on me. He blamed the injury. He said they couldn't be sure that I would ever get back to one hundred percent. He said I wasn't clicking with Powerball!

The same old racism.

If I went to Houston, I would end up with Sung again, and he would be the one to write about the next three years of my career. Carrie tried to comfort me, but somehow, even after the evidence of our entire Asian American lives, we had both been taken by surprise.

"Maybe it will be a cake," Carrie said.

I couldn't imagine racism as a cake.

Carrie said Sung and I were like star-crossed lovers. "At least the consolation prize is thirty million dollars."

On a whim, I asked my agent to see what he could get overseas.

Around that same time, Sung started calling me obsessively, maybe five times an hour every hour, and then calling Carrie too. Since it looked like I would have to get along with him, I finally picked up. "There better be a good reason for this," I said when I answered.

There was. Sung said a lawyer had called him because his adoptive father had willed him a single item. The lawyer wanted to know how Sung wished to receive it—pickup or delivery, like a pizza. That was how Sung found out his old man had died. They hadn't been in touch for years. After high school, his father had completely cut him off. Sung had put himself through college. Now, with one phone call, his entire childhood came back to him. He thought he was being punished, as if Ducky was not enough.

When he told me this, my heart started opening to him again. I couldn't help it. After everything that had happened between us, I was the one he called. On the other hand, he must have called me because I was his only Korean friend and the only one with any tie to adoption, even if it was secondhand. But I had thought of him as someone who could survive anything, simply because he would always do whatever he had to do to survive—his collapse touched me.

Sung had chosen delivery and had received in the mail a single manila envelope. This is when the calls began. He couldn't bring himself to open it. He wanted *me* to open it and report to him what it was.

When I got to the café, it was raining. He looked like he had rolled around in mud. It was caked to his knees. He couldn't remember how he had gotten that way. His hair was grayer than it had been when I last saw him, four months earlier. He put the envelope in front of me, which he had managed to keep dry.

"I'm sure the bastard just wanted me to know that he died and gave everything he had to someone else. That's the only reason he left me anything—so I would be notified."

I sighed and took the seat across from him. "What about Brit?" I asked. "Why didn't you have her do this for you? You're in love with her, aren't you?"

He said he had told Brit nothing about his adoptive father, since he didn't want her to see his adoption when she looked at him—that was how he put it. Maybe I was guilty of doing that. He said I probably knew more about his relationship with his dad now than anyone else in the world, unless his adoptive mom was still alive somewhere.

It was baffling and so lonely. He had trusted me with his past, yet he had thrown me under the bus to attack Powerball!

"I can't do this for you," I said. "I shouldn't have come."

"Please."

Didn't he have any other friends? But I knew he didn't or he would have called them. He had never truly trusted anyone he loved to love him back. That was why his adoptive father could hurt him so easily, because he was Sung's model for loving. I wanted Sung to see that there were other possibilities. He had, at one time, wanted to become like me.

I slit the envelope and looked inside. The entirety of his inheritance was a letter.

He swallowed a few times, as if his mouth had gone dry. Then he asked me to tell him what it said only if it was good news, which he assumed it wouldn't be, and not tell him if it was bad.

I shouldn't have looked, but I was too curious.

In the letter, his adoptive father had recorded everything he knew about Sung's adoption and birth family, the back-and-forth with the agency, the rare contact with Sung's birth mother, and then even a name, an address, a family register.

"I can't decide this for you," I said.

"Please."

"I don't know. I don't know if you would think this is good news or bad news." There was surely enough for him to find his Korean family, if he wanted.

"You do know," he said. "That's why I asked you."

He had no reason to think so. He just wanted it to be true in that moment.

His face drained, paling, emptying of blood.

I folded the letter back up and returned it to its envelope.

"We're not the same, Robert," I said.

He jerked back as if I had shot him. I remembered he had made that same movement the last time I had told him we were not the same.

"Listen," I said, "you'll read it eventually, and when you do, you tell me then what you think I should have done. I wonder if you'll think I did the right thing."

His jaw clenched and unclenched.

I really thought I would hear from him again, once we were both in Houston or whenever he finally read it—but I never did. That was the end of our subplot.

10. THE FATE OF BRIT YOUNG

Brit Young? I don't know what to tell you. Somehow, she got a judge to say Powerball! was an unfit father—it was the worst thing I ever saw a person do, and I don't even know how she managed—and she and Sung gave up their life in Houston and moved with the kids to Hollywood. Even Carrie stopped talking to her. Brit made her comeback as an actress. She won a role as a popular sitcom mother, twelve years older than her actual age, then ten years older, then eight, etc., who wanted the best for her kids yet was blamed for screwing up their lives. She was good at giving a look that seemed to say: *How is this possibly my fault?* Sometimes, Carrie and I spotted her on award shows. She was always alone. Either she had dropped Sung or he stayed home to watch the kids. I didn't want to know which. It broke my heart to see what losing the children did to Powerball!—or, rather, what it didn't do. He kept on balling as always, making the All-Star Game every year, almost getting MVP, then losing in the first round of the playoffs, while his family receded further and further from him. He never talked about them again. The year he retired, Brit won her first Emmy and gave a viral acceptance speech about trusting your feelings. "Your feelings are pretty smart," Carrie said with her, as if they had planned the speech together. "I can't believe she still remembers." In his retirement, Powerball! advocated for single fathers, not just for their rights but for changing how people saw them, because—he said—a man couldn't change his life until he could trade what he could do for what he couldn't. Eventually, his kids grew up and noticed his efforts; the two younger ones would even reconcile with him. The oldest would refuse contact with either parent—he would move to Paris and become a famous model, though part of that fame would always be who his parents were.

II. THE FATES OF WON LEE AND CARRIE KANG

In the end, instead of going to Houston, I left the NBA for the Korean Basketball League. It was a far easier decision than I thought it would be. I made less money but more than enough. I never had to deal with another question about whether or not I deserved the chances I got. Carrie and I got married before we left the States. She took a position with a Korean cable network and oversaw K-dramas full-time. The fans were disappointed—though once they found out that the Knicks had turned on me, the Asian American fans, at least, seemed to get it. They defended me against the pink-headed vultures on TV. What neither Carrie nor I expected was the fight our dads put up. Why "go back" to Korea, they wanted to know, when our families had sacrificed so much to give us American freedoms? We had to recruit our siblings to defend us. My sisters, as always, convinced my dad. Carrie's siblings tried, but her dad was more stubborn. Finally, her mom—who, as an adoptee, had grown up missing a country she couldn't remember—had to step in. She said that her husband didn't get a say at all, that the ability to see what was wrong with America was a freedom that Carrie herself had sacrificed for.

It's been six years since we moved here. The other day, while

Carrie's sister was visiting, she, Carrie, and their mom took our baby to the VIP baby class at Lotte Department Store. They sent me photos—sometimes the same photo in three different angles—of our baby hitting plastic butterflies with a plastic net, our baby toddling back and forth over a baby-sized bridge, our baby in a miniature strawberry costume unironically picking strawberries. With the last photo came a text that Carrie had something to tell me.

At last, we were at the point in our marriage where that phrase didn't scare me. I waited for them to get home. I knew what Carrie wanted to talk about: though the baby was only two, Carrie was convinced the girl was a genius. She wanted to make that label mean something.

All my experience told me that the idea of genius was a power play for people with money and privilege to insulate their children from other children—but becoming a father had made me want to give my kid whatever opportunities other people's kids could get. I wanted our kid to believe she could be anything she wanted to be—I wanted her to *be* anything she wanted to be.

"Kay should go on one of those baby-genius shows," Carrie said when she got home. "Should I try to get her on one? I know a PD who could help."

We had named her Kay after Carrie's nickname for her sister.

I asked Carrie if that was really what she wanted. Did she really want our child to be seen by so many people, to be observed and scrutinized?

But it was a different question in Korea than it would have been in America.

"Look at her!" Carrie's sister said.

The baby muttered to a stuffed tiger that it should poop on the potty and not in its (nonexistent) diaper. "Be a big girl, Tigey," she said. "Don't you know you're a big girl?"

"See?" Carrie said. "She knows she's a big girl."

When I arrived in Korea, I had thought that I would dominate the KBL, as the first Asian American basketball star, but there were a dozen players good enough for the chance I had gotten.

It was all about making what was possible *seem* possible.

"She knows she's a big girl," I said. "Sign her up."

12. CODA WITH BALL BOYS

There was only one time I ever heard any dirt on Powerball! that I believed. I heard it at the very end of my season in New York, a few days after the Knicks' third first-round playoff exit in as many years. We had lost at home in a sweep. The next morning, I went to the Garden early to shoot around by myself and consider what to do with my career. My knee was still healing, so I figured I'd take it easy, see if anyone was around to rebound. When I got there, a couple of ball boys were taking rainbow shots, a little competition to see who could hit the most. The balls made these high, beautiful arcs. The shots seemed full of mourning, like prayers. I kind of *had* to keep watching from the shadows. I didn't want to interrupt their pure love for the game. One of the ball boys was Asian and the other Latino, and they both had pretty good game and low-to-medium hops. The shots went in at about the same rate as the team's did in shootarounds, but flew higher and higher. They started a second game of horse, and I heard the Asian guy say, "They even pump them up this much in the off-season? He works out somewhere else in the summer, anyway—can't they let some air out?" The Latino said he'd once read that Magic had liked the balls pumped up to almost twice regulation since he was so tall and ran so hard.

"Twice?" the Asian one said. "No way. Someone would be onto that."

"People were onto it, sure. But who was going to stop Magic?"

They continued shooting. I turned and got out of there. The conspiracy jolted through me, like I had stuck a fork in a socket. Somehow, I had never noticed about the balls until that moment. Of *course* they were pumped up too much. Of *course* it gave Powerball! an edge and made the balls a little harder on me and anyone shorter and slower than he was. I didn't resent him. It just made me think there was a little extra to home-court advantage for the people who felt most at home there. Where was that home for me? How could I get the balls blown up as much or as little as I liked? On my way to the locker rooms, one of the security guards stopped me, and I had to convince him that I wasn't some random Asian dude sneaking into the Garden to see the Wonderkid but the actual sufferer of that nickname himself.

PART SEVEN
K-DRAMA
The Lonely, Shining Basketball Star

THE SECOND HALF OF A K-DRAMA

The second half of a K-drama is the show's danger zone. In the episodes just after the halfway point, a show is more likely both to lose its viewers and, in an attempt to keep them, to throw everything it can in the couple's way. If the first half of a K-drama is about falling in love, the second half is about holding on to love.

Here is where tropes like temporary amnesia, sudden illness, disapproving parents, etc. come in. The world keeps trying to shut down the couple, just when it is too late for them to go back to who they were before they loved each other. Their new selves, as lovers, have to deal with the problems of their old selves. One lover gets into a car accident and loses her memory of the other, and her lover has to win her over again, not as the person he used to be before he loved her, but now as the person her love has made him.

The typical K-drama is like the saying "You can never step in the same river twice." The couple has to cross their river over and over again, at different points, to affirm that they can cross it under any circumstances.

The following is the second half of one such K-drama, *The Lonely, Shining Basketball Star,* about a Korean American sportswriter and a KBL superstar.

I. THE MISUNDERSTANDING

Once upon a time in dramaland, a sportswriter and a basketball star fell in love. They fell in love despite the sportswriter having written the article that ended the star's career—and also *because* that article linked their fates together. When the sportswriter realized she was in love, she wished to revive the star's career, as if she could do so as easily as she had killed it. She thought it could work to write about his niece, how he had bet on the game to pay for the girl's hospitalization in America. If people knew why he had cheated, they would sympathize with him, as she had, and love him again, as she did.

But the star would not agree to this plan. He asked her not to write about his niece, as it would cause trouble for his brother. His brother's marriage would fall apart if his wife knew he had a secret daughter. The sportswriter didn't understand why her beloved would protect his brother instead of his own career. Especially since he had lost that career by trying to help his brother in the first place.

And so she wrote the article without telling him. She planned to take him out for dinner the night before, sit him down, and explain why she had done it. But the newspaper didn't wait.

Its social media account posted a teaser of the morning's story. The teaser shared only the information that would sell the most papers, which is to say: a former basketball star had a secret niece in a coma in a hospital in Maryland. There was no context included, none of the care the sportswriter had taken to protect the brother as much as she could. She had even risked her reputation to imply, in half-truths, that the brother didn't even know he had a daughter, that the girl had been born before his marriage, and that the news would catch him completely by surprise.

She had written the article in this way because she was in love.

A good misunderstanding is easily cleared up but impossible to take back.

Unaware of the newspaper's post, the sportswriter texted the star where to meet her. He replied that she should come out immediately and meet him at his parents' place instead.

This was a surprise, but it seemed like a good step forward in their relationship. She really did want to change his parents' impression of her. As far as she knew, they still thought of her as someone who had destroyed their son's career.

When she arrived at his parents' address, he was waiting outside the building, trying and failing to look inconspicuous, ducking his head so that he would seem shorter. It was adorable, she thought, like a puppy looking for a place to bury its bone. But as soon as he saw her, his eyes narrowed in a way she recognized, the way they had narrowed when he used to hate her.

"I can't believe you," he said. "You've ruined me twice now. Twice. This is how you treat someone you love?"

He held his phone in her face. As she read the social media posts, she remembered the three missed calls from her best friend in Korea while she was making herself up for dinner. Her heart pounded in her stomach.

"That isn't everything," she said desperately. "Wait until tomorrow. There's an entire article. This is just clickbait."

"But that's what the story amounts to," the star said. "Isn't it? That's the lede?"

"That isn't the lede I wrote."

"If you don't even know what you wrote, you shouldn't be a writer."

He said they couldn't afford to wait until tomorrow, she needed to meet his parents before they saw the article.

"When they read it," she said, "they'll see that I have your best interests—"

"They'll see," he said, "only that you exposed something that isn't any of your business, first ruining my reputation and then my brother's."

But could they really think that? Why would he want a woman like that to meet his parents?

He was already guiding her into the building. They spent the elevator ride in tense silence. He stepped straight out and up to the intercom beside his parents' door. Defiantly, she reached out to push the doorbell. Just before she could touch it, he pulled her back and held her tightly to him and said for the first time that he really loved her.

2. THE CHALLENGE OF THE PARENTS

Except his parents had seen the article already and refused to give their consent. A K-drama isn't won so easily. They said their son could never date her and was a fool for bringing her before them. "Don't you have any respect for your brother?" his father shouted. "If you're a brother, how could you even see her? If you're a man, how could you see her after the first article?"

The sportswriter stood up for him, tried to tell them that his brother had used him, but before she could go into all of that, he stopped her. That was the end of their relationship: the moment he silenced her in order to save his parents' pride in his brother.

The very next day, she took a job covering a Busan team, for less money, and though the star read the rest of the article and got everything back—his career, his brother, his money—she changed her number and never contacted him again.

It would be twenty games into the next season before the star's team played the Busan team, which was in another division. So for twenty games, he waited to see her again. Once more, he was adored by fans and teammates and coaches; he was celebrated as the best player over the first part of the season. He trained his hardest, played his hardest, waiting for her return. On the day of the game, he practically sprang with excitement. He started a dunk contest during the layup drill, putting on a show. From the moment the starting lineups were announced and the anthem sung, he spent every play looking for her. He didn't see her as he missed his spots, as he turned the ball over, as he threw up bricks and his team lost by thirty-five. Afterward, he faced the press eagerly, but she wasn't there either. To every question, he answered, "I'm sorry. It's my fault. I'll do better," answering her.

It turned out she had missed the game because another fan of his had attacked her. The fan had managed to stab her in the side before someone passed by and chased him off.

The next game, neither of them were there. The coach was frantic. The star disappeared for six games without a word to anyone. The sportswriter never returned.

3. THE TRIP ABROAD

Once upon a time in dramaland, a drama backtracked to show what happened to the sportswriter during those twenty games, how harrowed she'd been, stalked by the fan, how the police barely helped her—a woman and an American. She thought many times about calling the star, but each time, she would remember his family's rejection of her. She watched every game he played. She called her friends in America, who asked her to come home and start over. Then one night, after a late game, she let her guard down as she walked to her car, watching his game on her smartphone, and his fan rushed up behind her with a knife.

When the star found her in the hospital in Busan, he apologized for everything, and they restarted their romance, even though she couldn't get out of bed. But she wasn't really restarting. She wanted to spend some time with him before she would let him go for good. She had decided to return to America after all, to quit sportswriting altogether. To do something she could do on her own.

As soon as the star went back to his team, she had herself transferred to the hospital in Maryland where his niece was in a coma, where she could watch over the girl, and she told everyone she knew not to let him know where she had gone. She left his life completely.

She recovered in that hospital, and then she worked in DC at different jobs, taking night courses in filmmaking. She noticed when the star's PSA about fan behavior went viral across Korea and even caused NBA players to make similar PSAs that caught fire all over YouTube. But she didn't call or email him or contact him at all. Her only connection to his life now was when she checked in on his niece sometimes. She started her thesis project, a short film about white men who play sports video games and get used to the control of moving around black bodies—who ask, "Who do you play?" as a shorthand for ownership. When the film made the festival rounds, a surprise favorite, she got called up to advise on the latest NBA video games. It was part of a DEI project, but she did it for money and worked on another film idea on the side.

Two years passed. The end of a K-drama is ruthless with time.

Finally, the star got word that the sportswriter was no longer a writer but worked at a video game company. Someone had found the short film, of course, and tracked her down. Right away, the star tried to figure out how to join the NBA. He was at the top of the KBL then, MVP two years running—he had poured his life into basketball to keep from missing her constantly. And still, he couldn't get NBA teams interested; they made him work out like an undrafted teenager. He did so without complaint and dominated every category but quickness. He was in his prime and he knew his body was about to decline. In the KBL, he could play another five or six seasons of championships and records—instead he chased a spot in the NBA.

Finally, one team "took a chance on him," and soon he was starting, putting up the numbers of a key role player, a third option. He wasn't an All-Star, but he was voted one by fans across Asia, so he was able to play two minutes in a game dominated by players he had watched and learned from in the KBL. His pride wasn't hurt. He was done caring about pride. Those two minutes were all he needed. Because he was an All-Star, he would have the opportunity to do the motion capture for his video game avatar, as every All-Star did—that was what he had worked for. He would see the reporter again, which they both knew, which they both had waited for and hoped for and dared to believe in despite their different and distant lives. They would know love again, but this time, they would know what they were getting into.

This is our story's frame of reference. Now go back and read the book again.

ACKNOWLEDGMENTS

I wrote the first draft of this book in two halves. The first half is indebted to Robert Boswell's excellent prompts. The second half, I wrote while my wife was dying of cancer, much of it from beside her hospital bed. I saved K because I couldn't save my wife. Writing this book was an exercise in wanting to live.

I am grateful, as always, for my friend and reader, Kirstin Chen. I have the great fortune to work with my dream team of Vivian Lee and Ayesha Pande. I could not ask for a better editor and agent. Thanks to Cathy Chung, Laura van den Berg, and Kristen Arnett for the kind words that grace the dust jacket. Many, many thanks to Lena Little and everyone else at Little, Brown who helped send this book into the world. Lastly, love to all and any who communed with Won and Carrie, whether you know you did or not.

My kiddos—thank you for being alive. Thank you for growing up so well. Your mom would have been so proud.

ABOUT THE AUTHOR

Matthew Salesses is the author of the national bestseller *Craft in the Real World,* the 2021 finalist for the PEN/Faulkner Award for Fiction *Disappear Doppelgänger Disappear,* and two other novels. Adopted from Korea, he has written about adoption, race, and Asian American masculinity in *The Best American Essays 2020*, NPR's *Code Switch,* the *New York Times* blog *Motherlode,* and *The Guardian,* among other media outlets. *BuzzFeed* has named him one of thirty-two Essential Asian American Writers. He lives in New York City, where he is an Assistant Professor of Writing at Columbia University.